The Mark of the Coven

Eileen Roof

Dark Shadow Press—Avalon, CA
ISBN: 979-8-9880279-0-4
eBook ISBN: 979-8-9880279-1-1
Library of Congress Control Number: 2023904947
Title: *The Mark of the Coven*
Author: Eileen Roof
Digital distribution | 2023
Paperback | 2023

This is a work of fiction. The characters, names, incidents, places, and dialogue are products of the author's imagination, and are not to be construed as real.

Dedication

For Rebecca who encouraged me to share
my story

Chapter 1

Darkness spread across the ground like a blanket, rushing towards Lexi as her feet pounded against the moss laden ground. She raced as fast as she could towards Eliden, her tiny village. Night was falling quickly, and she had strayed too far, searching for herbs to replenish her dwindling supply. She was in the Grey Wood, so named for the grey trees that populated the area. Their leaves were a sparkling silver with bits of red and green thrown in here and there. They were a beautiful sight. The ground was lush with undergrowth and smelled of earth and moss, which would normally comfort and relax her. This was her favorite place. She had done little traveling, but she was certain nothing in all of Nivia could compare.

Lexi let her instincts guide her, knowing that she was going to cut it close. Not only was she going to be late for dinner, but the danger the woods held had been drilled into her all her life. Lexi was a mage and at 19, the perfect age for a vampyre coven to capture and turn. As an adult, she had unlocked her full potential and, being so young, the power in her blood would temporarily double or triple the biter's abilities. It only took one bite to turn a victim and there was no way she wanted to become one of the cursed. A turned mage kept some of their abilities. The older the mage, the less they retained, and the rumors say that cursed mages belong to the coven of the vampyre that turns them. Nope, not going to happen. Lexi did not belong to anyone.

The surrounding trees were starting to thin, and glints of light from the village flashed in front of her. There was an ominous chill from the approaching darkness as it kissed her skin while she raced toward safety. The sound of her breathing was all she could hear as she struggled to force air into her lungs. Her muscles were on fire and all she wanted to do was stop and breathe, but if she did, she knew she was a goner. She could see the shimmering line caused by the protective wards that kept the biters out of her village. Once she crossed it, she would be safe. At least she'd be safe from the biters. Her father was a whole different story. As she neared the line, she felt the tingle of danger that told her a biter was on her heels. Lexi cursed and tried to get more speed out of her screaming leg muscles. Just as she was about to make freedom and cross the line into safety, she felt the cold dead vice like grip grab her arm and start to pull her away from the glistening line of safety in front of her.

Lexi let out a terrified scream and whirled toward the pale biter who had hold of her and sent a blast of power from her free hand straight at his chest. The stunning blow caught him right in the middle of his chest, causing all of his muscles to go limp, freeing Lexi and sending the biter flying a few feet backwards. She didn't hesitate, whirling back towards the village; she fled towards safety. Hearing a frustrated growl, she didn't bother to look back as the biter regained his mobility. If she had been even a foot farther from home, she would not have escaped.

Her home sat close to the edge of the Grey Wood and as she rounded the corner of the wall that circled her yard, she almost ran straight into her father, who had his sword and was running towards her. He was tall, just over six feet, with black hair and brown eyes. It was impossible to mistake him for anything other than a warrior. Commander Byron Vaughn may be semi-retired, but he was still deadly.

As soon as she was within reach, he enveloped her in a tight bear hug, crushing her and causing what little air she had managed to get into her lungs to immediately vacate her body. He must have heard her scream when the biter grabbed her and rushed to her rescue.

"Do you have any idea what you have put me through?" he roared, as he crushed her tightly to his chest.

"Can't breathe," Lexi croaked.

"What happened?" her father asked, only slightly loosening his hold as he turned them towards home.

"I lost... track... of time... collecting... and raced the night... back home. Biter caught me at the ward line... and I blasted him," Lexi panted out her explanation. She had contemplated leaving out the last bit, but she knew he had heard her scream and would be even angrier if she didn't tell him everything.

Her father growled and released her as they neared the front door of their two-story home.

"Byron, is everything ok? I see you have your sword. Did I miss something?" Mavis, their next-door neighbor, called out to them. Mavis was about 102 and deaf as a log.

Byron waved at her. "Just my daughter trying to take years off my life by scaring me to death," he roared at her. "Nothing to worry about."

Mavis smiled and waved as they headed inside.

Lexi collapsed into a plush chair in the living room, still trying to recover from her ordeal. Whiskers, her grey tabby, immediately jumped into her lap, curling up in a ball and purring loudly. The action comforted her as the realization of how close she came to a fate she was sure was worse than death hit her hard. Lexi started to shake and fought back tears. Her father's heavy footsteps moved from the kitchen to the living room. He stopped in front of her.

"Are you ok?" he asked in a soft voice.

"Yes," Lexi whispered.

"What you did was reckless, and I wasn't kidding about how scared I was that I might lose you." Her father sighed and shook his head. "You have been warned about the dangers of being outside of the wards at night. I don't know what else I can do to get it through your head. Those things took your mother. I will not let them have you, too."

Her father's copper eyes flashed with anger and Lexi winced. If he got going, there would be no stopping him.

"I'm sorry. I won't let it happen again." She looked up with pleading eyes and hoped he believed her.

"I have heard that before and I know you don't mean to be reckless." Her father stared at her, clenching and unclenching his jaw. "Right now, dinner is ready. Go wash up and come eat. We will discuss what your new restrictions are after dinner." Her father stomped off to the kitchen.

Lexi eased the cat from her lap and stood, her muscles protesting the movement. She went to the small downstairs bathroom to wash. As she looked at her reflection in the mirror, she noticed the contrast of colors.

Her face was pale and there was color high in her cheeks. Her hair was black as a raven's, long and straight with a deep purple stripe that ran down the right side with smaller strips woven throughout. The color matched her eyes. Every mage had similar hair and eyes. The colors varied, indicating their specialty. Hers was extremely rare. Not only could she do everything a basic mage could do, she was transcended and could move between dimensions. She also had visions that gave her splitting headaches. At 5 foot 6 inches and 125 pounds she was the scariest mage in her village, all she had to do was smile and people started shaking and moving away quickly. She had gotten that reaction from people all her life and didn't understand why until she had gone to school to learn control and found out what the color meant.

Lexi shook her head. Now wasn't the time to get lost in her thoughts. She turned on the water and washed her hands. As she glanced down, she noticed a bracelet on her wrist that hadn't been there before. It had a woven black band and a silver charm. The charm was an eye with a dagger through it, the dagger had a purple stone on the pommel. There was no clasp, and it wasn't loose enough to slip onto or off of her wrist. It was pretty, but she knew the only way it could have appeared was from the biter. She immediately tried to cut it off and found that the band could not be cut. She tried to burn it off with the candle that was on the counter, and that had no effect, either. Panicking, she tried a spell to shrink and found that the bracelet shrank with her like it was part of her.

"DAD!!" Lexi yelled as she rushed to the kitchen. "I think the biter marked me! This bracelet just appeared, and I can't get it off."

Lexi shoved her wrist in front of her father's face, frantic with worry over what it might mean. Her father grabbed her wrist and moved it so that he could inspect the bobble.

He pulled at the band and tried to cut it with his knife, having the same luck she had. Then he inspected the charm and paled as he realized what the charm meant.

"This is a tracking charm. The only one that can remove it is the one that put it in place. This charm will tell the tracker where you are at all times. It also implies that you belong to a vampyre coven. Any vampyre not of that coven that attempts to bite you will meet a very painful death," he explained.

Lexi took a sharp breath and stared at her father with wide eyes. "W-what? H-how could they mark me without turning me?" she stammered, sinking into her chair at the table.

Her father sighed and placed a plate with steak, potatoes and green beans in front of her. "Eat," he said.

"Eat? Eat!? What do you mean eat? I have been marked..." She hysterically waved her hands.

Her father held up his hand to stop her tirade. "There is nothing we can do about the mark right now. Tomorrow we will contact the High Warlock and see what he has to say," he said, calmly.

Lexi huffed and dug in. She was starving and knew that arguing was pointless at this point. After dinner, she did the dishes, fed the cat and put away her herbs. Then she showered and went to bed, hoping that when she woke in the morning, she would find answers to her questions.

Chapter 2

Lexi woke to the sun streaming into her bedroom. She felt groggy, and her entire body felt heavy. She'd had weird dreams. All she could remember was that she was somewhere dark and the biter that had marked her was there, but the rest of the dream had already faded. Climbing out of bed, she dressed in jeans and a tank top, then headed downstairs to find her father.

"Well, it's about time. I thought you were going to sleep the day away," her father said. He smiled at her from the sofa, turning his mobile in his hand nervously.

Lexi froze at the bottom of the stairs, staring at him. Her father didn't get nervous. He was a fighter. Before the biters had taken her mother, her father had been the commander of the White Garrison, a group of battle-hardened warriors that protected the many beings that called Nivia home. The majority of the fighting forces of Nivia were human, as were most of the people that made up the outlying cities. There are a few mages that choose to fight alongside those that prove themselves worthy of joining the

White Garrison. The garrison consists of 7 teams, 1 general, 5 warriors, all having reached at least sergeant level, and 6 mages one for each of the sanctioned magi specialties. It was the Circle of Magi's elite fighting force. Each faction has a similar group, each charged with protecting their faction from the others. They mainly stayed in their factions keep, ready to be deployed at a moment's notice. Byron Vaughn had been in charge of the entire garrison before he married her mother and they moved to Elidan. So, his nervousness scared her.

"You're nervous. What's wrong?" Lexi sat in the chair she had been in the night before, waiting for whatever bomb he was about to drop on her.

"We have to travel to Night City." He wouldn't look her in the eye as he said it. He cleared his throat and picked at the arm of the sofa, avoiding her.

"Why?" she asked. Confused and a little scared.

"I spoke with the high warlock this morning and told him what happened. He said the only way you might get the mark removed is to appeal to the royal house of the coven that marked you. In your case, it will be the house of the All-Seeing Eye," he replied. His response came out in a flat, almost defeated tone.

"You told me that travel to Night City is forbidden for Transcended, and if I ever go there, I can't return home." Lexi could feel her panic rise. Night City was a haven of sorts: each Vampyre coven had a royal house there, along with the house of Magi. Each faction had a place in Night City where their people would be safe from harm by the other factions. Then there was the heart of the city where the factionless resided, the underbelly as it was, where anything goes. People disappeared and there were no rules.

Her father winced at that and turned a bit red. "Technically, it's not forbidden by the council. It's just frowned upon," he said. Giving her a sheepish look. "Please don't be mad. You were obsessed with the city when you were younger, and I had to do something to stop you from getting it into your head to go there."

Lexi was shocked her father had lied to her. He never lied. Even when it was hard to hear and even harder to say he spoke the truth, he never tried to sugarcoat things or downplay danger. He was always brutally honest. Still, she understood. "I'm not mad. A little shocked, but not mad," she said with a sigh. The relieved look on her father's face almost made her tear up.

"So, I have to go to Night City and do what exactly?" Lexi asked, looking at her father, squaring her shoulders and preparing herself for the task ahead.

"We will be going to the city and petitioning for an audience with the royal house of the

All-Seeing Eye for a removal of marking. As far as the High Warlock knows, there has never been such a petition, so he doesn't know exactly what it will entail," he said.

Lexi sighed, "I will be doing this on my own." She held up her hand, like he had the night before, to stop the tirade he was drawing in a deep breath to deliver.

He let the breath out in a heavy sigh and motioned for her to continue.

"I need to do this on my own. I am an adult now and you have a new batch of cadets to train. You can't just leave and say, sorry, not sure when I'll be back. This is a sword. The pointy end goes toward the bad guy."

He chuckled at that.

"I got myself into this mess and as much as I would love to hide behind you, I can't let you fix everything my whole life," she said.

Her father's eyes glistened as he took a couple of breaths. "I can't lose you. There is a chance that if you go, you might not return."

Her eyes teared up, and she moved over to the couch to hug her father. "I know it's scary. I am terrified, but I have to do this, and you need to have faith that I will come back. It's not like I will be out of touch. We can chat on the phone, and I will keep you updated, I promise."

He hugged her tightly and nodded. "Okay, but at the first sign of trouble, I will come running."

Lexi gave a small chuckle. "Maybe not the first sign," she said with a grin. "You know I always find trouble."

Her dad laughed, "Yeah ok maybe you 're right but the 2nd sign for sure." He let her go and she went to pack for the trip.

Not knowing how long she would be gone, she packed almost all of her wardrobe. She had charmed a small backpack to be lightweight and carry several suitcases worth of clothes. Sometimes, being a mage rocked.

With her bag in hand, she went to go have lunch with her dad before her train left for the city. He'd made sandwiches and opened chips and set out some fruit. There was enough food on the table for 4 or 5 people.

"Umm dad I can't eat this much and last time I checked, you were still only eating for one as well." Lexi joked with him as she grabbed some grapes from the bowl.

He just smiled at her as the doorbell rang. She scowled at the door and went to answer it. Standing on the stoop were her best friends Max and Tia, her only friends really, but that's ok with these two as your besties. You didn't need anyone else.

Max was tall, 6'6" slim but not scrawny, with auburn hair that had fiery red and yellow streaks through it. His hair always resembled the sun at sunset to Lexi. She loved the colors and hated the way he kept it short and spiked. His eyes were a vibrant red with yellow pupils that seemed to glow against his tan skin, it was obvious from a mile off that his specialty was fire not only was he a fire mage but he was a master fire mage and if he chose to he could go far in the fire guild, Max had a movie star quality with his bright smile and flippant attitude.

Tia was a bit taller than Lexi 5'7 with ashen hair that had mint green streaks through it and caramel skin that made the green of her eyes seem more vibrant she was the bubbly one of the group and always seemed happy with a bounce in her step and a smile on her face being near her was almost rejuvenating. Not surprising, since her specialty marked her as a healer and herbalist.

Lexi squeed and hugged them both. "I thought you were on a trip across Nivia exploring all the wonders of the land," she said quoting the brochure.

"Please, without you, it was positively boring, so we decided to return early," Max said. Returning her hug and moving toward the food.

Tia giggled as she joined him. "Yes, and Max setting the tour guides' hair on fire had nothing to do with that."

"You what?" Lexi exclaimed.

Gaping at Max while her father looked at him, perplexed, with a sandwich halfway to his mouth.

Max just shrugged and popped a chip into his mouth. "The man was an insufferable ass who apparently thought we were unruly teens that needed stupid rules to follow, so I acted out my anger. Besides, I didn't set it on fire. It was just an illusion. Not my fault. He pissed himself and jumped into the river."

Lexi laughed, it felt good to laugh, then her laughing turned to crying as her emotions got the better of her and it took a good 10 minutes before she regained control enough to explain to her friends what had happened to her and what she had to do to fix her new problem.

"We will go with you." Max stated flatly. Which immediately got a chorus of no's from Lexi and her father with an excited squee from Tia.

"No. NO! Absolutely not!" Lexi yelled, looking from one friend to the other.

Max just grinned at her and shook his head. "Lexi, love, you know we can't turn down an adventure. Besides, where you go, we go. I suggest you stop arguing and accept the fact that we will be joining you in this endeavor." Max held Lexi's gaze, practically daring her to try to argue as Tia bounced in her seat next to him.

Lexi's father looked from Max to Lexi and sighed in resignation, "Safety in numbers, it might be better if they accompanied you."

Lexi sat down hard, shocked a bit by her father's statement. "You planned this," she accused. Pinning her father with an angry stare. "You knew they were coming. You made extra food. You...." Lexi couldn't finish. She just stared at him, feeling a bit hurt and betrayed.

Her dad shook his head. "No, I didn't plan this. I knew they were coming, yes. Max texted this morning asking if they could come surprise you, and I suggested lunch, but that was all. You know I would never intentionally put your friends in harm's way, but I am well aware that much like you when they have made up their minds to do something, there is no stopping them." His statement was gentle and sincere.

Lexi nodded slowly, allowing her hurt to fade a bit.

Tia beamed and wiggled a bit in her seat, her excitement plain for all to see. "So, when do we leave? How do we get there? Do I need to pack anything special? Where exactly are we going? Should...."

"Tia!" Max said, putting a hand on her arm, stopping her rapid-fire questions. "One question at a time, please." Max gave her arm a gentle squeeze and smiled at her softly before letting go and joining the others in a discussion to answer all those questions and any others she might think up.

Chapter 3

It was just getting dark as they headed for the train station. The station itself was interesting, since the only stop was Night City. It had to accommodate all factions. There was a Warded section for those that wanted or needed protection from the biters and wolves, with sections for each faction to accommodate their specific needs. As the massive engine roared into view, you could see people and creatures shuffling into lines. The train came to a screeching stop with a soft whooshing of doors and a small stream of people exiting and shuffling towards the designated exits. The lines slowly started to move as people boarded.

Lexi turned to her father and gave him a hug. "I promise to keep you updated. Please take good care of Whiskers," she said.

Byron hugged his daughter tightly, not wanting to let go. After a few moments, he sighed and pulled away. "I will, and you better. You have the Retractable I gave you and the dagger?"

He looked her over as she gave him a watery smile and held up the necklace, she wore with the hilt of a retractable sword attached. To the naked eye, it appeared to be a large cross with a gem in the middle and smaller gems going up to the top. If she clasped it, pushing in the smaller gems and the large gem at the same time, a 3' blade would shoot out. It was a slender but strong sword, made by Elven blacksmiths. It was a very sturdy, almost unbreakable blade of Elven silver. Lexi turned and held up her boot to show the matching digger secured in its sheath. The dagger was sharper than a razor and enchanted to only cut those that meant to do the bearer harm.

He smiled a bit sheepishly and fussed over everyone, making sure they had all they needed.

Max gently touched Lexi's shoulder and said, "It's time."

Almost everyone else had boarded, and they needed to go if they were going to make tonight's train. The train only ran once a night and if you missed it, you had to wait for the next night. The ride was about 12 hours. The trains were automated and ran constantly, but there was no way to run more than one per track.

Lexi nodded and gave her dad one last hug before she allowed Max to assist her in boarding the warded train car. Max helped Tia up behind her and then joined them in looking for an unoccupied room to claim as theirs for the trip, The car they found had plush cream-colored sofas that would double as a nice place to nap if one got tired during the long ride.

Lexi sat on one sofa while Tia and Max took the other one. Tia immediately curled up against Max's side and he placed a protective arm around her, helping her get comfortable. Lexi smiled a bit at them. They weren't an 'official' couple, however Lexi had never seen either of them show interest in anyone else.

Tia had been her friend for as long as she could remember, and Max had decided he was going to join their group shortly after moving to Eliden. There had been a bully trying to force them to hand over their lunch money. He had knocked Tia down and made her cry. Lexi was doing her best to shield her from any further harm when Max suddenly appeared in front of them. Blocking the bully's access as he calmly explained that he didn't approve of the bully's actions. At 8 years old, he was tall for his age and a bit scary to look at with the vibrant colors of his eyes and hair. The bully had tried to punch him and Max fast as a snake had spun and flipped him to the ground, pinning him with his foot to the boy's throat. At that point, a teacher had come rushing up yelling for Max to let the boy go. Max had shrugged and done as he was told, saying that if she wanted to yell at someone, perhaps she should start with the boy that had hit Tia. He then kneeled down in front of them and, in the gentlest voice Lexi had ever heard, asked Tia if she was ok. Tia had locked gazes with him, and they had been inseparable ever since.

Max caught her smile and returned it with one of his own. "You may want to get some rest too since we have no real idea of what this adventure holds for us," he said.

Lexi nodded. "I know but I am a bit amped I never in my wildest dreams thought I would be going to the city."

Max nodded in understanding. "Me either, but with you two as my companions, I have learned to expect the unexpected and roll with it."

Max and Lexi chatted for an hour or so about the past and what might be in store for them. It didn't take long before Lexi felt her eyes get heavy and then she was asleep and dreaming of a dark, dangerous place with a pale stranger intent on sucking her blood and turning her into one of his pets. The last thing she remembered hearing before she woke with a start was a whispered, "I'll be waiting for you in Night City."

Lexi came awake, trying to calm herself. The dream had felt real, and her body was still heavy with sleep. She could smell food and spied Tia entering the car with 2 white bags that appeared to be stuffed with goodies. Max was sprawled on the sofa across from her and appeared to be in about the same shape she was. As Lexi sat up, she saw him run a hand across his face and through his hair. Then he looked at Tia and frowned.

"You left the car? Without waking me? The fact that you were able to exit without my noticing aside, what were you thinking? You know that during travel is one of the most dangerous times for a woman to be alone!" Max was getting worked up, his anger was almost a physical thing in the car with them, and much to Lexi's surprise Tia responded with anger of her own.

Tia never got angry. She was always happy and bubbly. "It's nice of you to finally notice that I have grown into a woman," Tia stated. Dumping the bags onto the small table and setting the drink holder that Lexi was sure held 3 cups of coffee next to them. "However, I am not your property. I can come and go from wherever I like whenever I like without permission or an escort. I am also quite capable of taking care of myself." Tia hmphed and crossed her arms as she flopped down on the sofa next to Lexi.

Lexi looked from one friend to the other, a bit shocked at Tia's display, and promptly excused herself, jumping up and rushing into the small bathroom that adjoined their car.

Max watched Lexi make her escape and slowly kneeled in front of Tia, taking her hands in his. He gently uncrossed her arms, caught and held her gaze. With his height, they were eye to eye with her sitting on the sofa and him kneeling in front of her.

"Tia, I have been in love with you since I was 8 years old. I fell in love with you the moment I saw you. I have waited patiently for you to decide that you love me, too. There has never been and will never be any other woman in my life more important to me than you. I am sorry if my protectiveness makes you feel oppressed in any way. I would never presume to own you or feel that I have any rights to dictate your freedoms," he said soft and firm.

Tia sniffed, and Max gently brushed a soft tear from her face. That soft, gentle touch was Tia's undoing. She flung herself off the sofa and into his arms. Max caught her and held her tightly as she sobbed into his shoulder. It took her a few moments to collect herself.

"How come you never told me?" Tia whispered, pulling back slightly to look into his eyes.

Max chuckled and gave her a grin. "Sweetheart, it was plainly obvious to everyone. Well, almost everyone, I guess."

Lexi hollered from the bathroom. "Yep. Head over heels from day one."

"Thank you, peanut gallery." Tia hollered back, making note of the thin walls that separated the rooms. With a deep breath, Tia wrapped her arms around Max's neck and kissed him senseless. She hoped that kiss would tell him everything she couldn't put into words. When the kiss finally ended, they were both breathing hard. Tia touched her forehead to his. "Just to be perfectly clear, I love you too, and you are forgiven," Tia said a bit breathless. She felt a bit vulnerable and exposed, but at the same time, happy and free.

Max smiled a bright smile and kissed her gently, setting her back on the sofa she had launched herself from. He stood and moved to knock on the door of the restroom. "It's all clear. You missed a great show." Max looked at Tia and winked. She blushed and grinned back at him.

Lexi sauntered out of the bathroom. "It's about time. I'm starving. What's for breakfast?"

Tia immediately grabbed the bags and unloaded the contents onto the table. "I got breakfast burritos and fruit cups and, of course, coffee."

They ate in a comfortable silence, watching the sky start to lighten, then suddenly they were immersed in darkness as the train sped into a tunnel.

The automatic lights slowly flared to life, and a computer-generated voice sounded throughout the entire train. "All passengers, please be sure to dispose of any garbage you may have accumulated during your trip; We will arrive in Night City in approximately 10 mins. All night dwellers, please note the sun has risen and for your safety, we ask that you use the tunnels provided to reach your desired destination."

Chapter 4

10 long minutes later, the train screeched to a halt, opening its doors to allow the passengers onboard to exit and the new ones to board.

Max jumped down onto the platform first, making sure it was safe. He looked around quickly, then turned to help Tia down. He gave her a quick squeeze, then turned to help Lexi. The 3 of them moved toward the exit marked Circle of Magi, moving from the dim tunnel to the bright morning light. They paused to let their eyes adjust.

Max kept a protective arm around Tia trying to make it appear natural and loving, but Lexi could see the tenseness in his shoulders and the way he kept scanning the area, making sure that there were no immediate dangers in their path. Max being an enigma had not been satisfied with just being a fire welding bad ass, he had trained in several different types of martial arts and even convinced Lexi's father to allow him to take the summer training program for warriors 3 years in a row. Not only could he wield fire as an offensive or defensive weapon, but he could also wield any weapon that he got his hands on. The man was deadly, and she was happy he was on her side.

About 10 feet in front of them was an archway with a booth in the middle showing a bored-looking earth mage inside giving directions to the mages that had come in on the trains. There were 7 trains in all, one for each of the outlying villages. On either side of the booth, there were warriors standing guard in case any trouble should arise. It intrigued Lexi to notice that there weren't any wards. Once she had exited the train, there were nothing but simple ropes and signs to guide people to where they needed to go.

The Circle was supposed to be a safe place for mages to hone their craft, but to Lexi it just seemed to be a place for the purists to live in peace. Although it was allowed for mages to marry those not of their specialty, it was highly disdained. Mages that married out of their specialty were not permitted to reside inside the circle. They could visit, however, if they chose to marry or live with someone not of their specialty, they had to live in either Night City or one of the outlying areas.

Finally, it was their turn. They had been last in line. Lexi stood behind Max and Tia while they waited in line, but now that it was their turn, she moved to stand next to Max as they approached the desk.

"Fire mage first castle to the right. Healer, second castle to the left. Just look for your colors." The mage said in a snooty, nasally dismissive tone. Then he glanced at her, went pale and hit a button, slamming down some sort of protective shield as he shouted, "YOU! YOUR KIND ISN'T ALLOWED HERE!" And with that, all hell broke loose. A very loud alarm sounded. Warriors started pouring out of the keep that was housed next to the building. The jerk at the desk fled through an escape portal and Max put up a fire shield, circling the three of them and keeping the warriors back. They turned toward the sound of pounding feet, putting the booth behind them. Max moved, so that he was slightly in front of Tia, using his body to shield hers.

"Fire mage, lower the barrier. You will not be harmed." The command sounded from somewhere in front of where Lexi stood. She could see nothing but the flames in front of her and had to shield her eyes from the glare.

"I think not," Max shouted back, looking in the direction of where the owner of the voice should be standing. "You have at least 50 nervous trigger happy, shiny new warriors, all pointing crossbows or pistols at my friend."

Lexi raised an eyebrow at Max. He could see through the flames. How awesome was that? He gave her a grin and a wink.

"Men rest arms," came the response from the other side of the wall.

Lexi expected Max to lower his shield, but nothing happened. She gave him a curious look and waited.

"Fire wielder, we have lowered our weapons. Please disperse your wall of fire."

Max snorted, "Look again, big guy, you have 2 warriors ready to shoot the second I comply."

Lexi's mouth formed a surprised O as she realized what was happening on the other side of the wall. She took a small step back and found Tia's hand squeezing it with hers. Tia hadn't moved from where Max had put her.

"My apologies, fire wielder I hadn't noticed. Remove them, take them to the keep. I will address them later." Movement was heard from the other side of the wall, then a door slamming.

Max lowered his wall, keeping a sharp eye out for anyone who may try to harm them. "Maximilious Varous III, you may call me Max." Max addressed the warrior at the front of the line.

"Anon Bright," replied the blond, muscular, very tall man in front of them. "I apologize for the rude welcome. Please, if you could explain to me exactly what caused the alarm, I would appreciate it greatly."

"I believe it was because of me." Lexi took a small step forward.

Anon turned to her and looked her up and down. "I see, and what did you do to warrant such a response?" Anon appeared to genuinely not understand the situation. There was absolutely no hate or fear in his eyes.

Lexi laughed. She couldn't help it. The whole situation was preposterous. "I was born," was her reply. "Do you really not know what I am?" she asked, not believing that there could be a being in all of Nivia that didn't know how to spot a transcended mage.

"You're a mage, a transcended mage, I believe. This is the Circle of Magi. I fail to see the issue," he said.

His response shocked her. There were very few people that flippant about her specialty. Lexi smiled. "Even in the Magi community, I am not welcome. My specialty is looked down upon and feared. Most people are afraid that I will open a portal to another dimension and shove them into it, or that my ability to see a person's past and potential future makes them think I will start shouting their deepest secrets. Many believe that I am evil, I'm not but most don't give me the chance to explain that I can't simply see a person's deepest secrets and if I wanted to read someone, I would need their permission, the process requires cooperation between the reader and the person being read. There are a lot of rules to my specialty, some imposed by the council, and some imposed by me."

Lexi lifted her shoulder in a halfhearted shrug. This was her life, and she was used to being treated as an outsider. Being able to explain she wasn't a threat was nice, but she didn't expect anything to change.

"I see," Anon replied in his calm commanding tone. "What brings you to the circle? If you knew you most likely wouldn't be welcome, why come?"

He cocked his head a bit and waited for her to answer. The troops behind him hadn't moved and were watching the exchange with interest. Max was being his vigilant self, ready to pounce if any violence erupted and Tia was trying to get a better view but was being held in place by Max's strong arm.

"I was summoned here to meet with the high warlock," she said.

Lexi's reply caused a sharp intake of breath from the crowd of warriors surrounding them.

Anon nodded. "Troops dismissed," he commanded, and waited until they vacated the area. Two remained to take their posts near the booth. "Please allow me to escort you. Miss?"

Lexi blushed. She hadn't even told him her name. How rude. "Sorry I'm Alexia Vaughn. Lexi for short. You have met Max."

Max nodded.

"And this is Mylitia Abberwood. She prefers Tia."

Anon gave Tia a smile, taking note of the way Max was protecting her. He gave a slight bow and swept his arm towards the entrance to the circle.

Lexi nodded and proceeded him through the entrance. Tia and Max followed her, with Anon bringing up the rear. Lexi crossed through the archway and stopped short. The circle was huge. There were 7 massive castles; they formed a circle, each having a path that led to large gate entrances and each painted a different color. The rainbow indicated where each mage faction belonged.

Nivia seemed to have a thing for color and the number 7 Lexi didn't know why. In the middle of the courtyard there was an enormous statue showing a mage holding a spell book and a wand, ready to cast a spell. Strictly speaking, mages didn't use wands, they all had one but were only used for large spells.

"Wow," Tia said, linking her arm through Lexi's.

"Impressive." Max said from behind them. Apparently, Max had released Tia, deeming it safe now that the battalion of warriors was no longer a threat. Lexi suspected another conversation about Max's overprotectiveness was in their future.

Anon moved in front of them. To the left was a driveway with several black SUVs. He headed towards them, pointing a small remote at one. It chirped, and the engine started. He held the passenger door open for Lexi while Max helped Tia into the back before sliding in next to her. Anon made sure she was secure before he closed the door and jogged around the front of the vehicle to take his place in the driver's seat. He placed the car in gear and headed for the tunnel made by the legs of the statue. There were a few other cars moving about and even a bus, but for the most part, the roads were empty.

"The faction castles are easily identified to the right. You have red for fire, copper for earth, and yellow for light. To the left you have blue for water, green for herb, and white for wind." He pointed out the different castles as he drove.

"At the head of the circle is the castle that belongs to the Circle's council. The high warlock should be there." He pointed. The 7th castle came into view as they passed through the legs of the statue. It was larger than the other 6 with no colors showing.

They came to a stop in front of a similar archway to the one they passed through to enter the circle. Anon cut the engine and jumped out. Max slid out of the vehicle and Tia slid out next to him. Instead of waiting for someone to open her door and not even thinking about what type of circus it might cause, Lexi opened her door and jumped out. She saw the 2 guards stiffen and the girl at the booth turn pale and glance at the panic button.

"Miss Alexia Vaughn has been summoned for an audience with the High Worlock," Anon stated as he stepped in front of her.

"O-of course," the girl stammered as she stood on shaky legs in front of them. "He is waiting in the council chambers for his guests. Would you like me to escort you?" she asked.

The poor girl would probably faint if they said yes, Lexi thought as she watched the girls' yellow eyes dart between them.

"That will not be necessary. I am well aware of the layout of this castle." Anon gave the girl a curt nod. "Miss Lexi," he said as he gently cupped her elbow, turning toward the massive doors being opened by the 2 guards. Once the doors were opened, the guards stood at attention until the group passed, then they closed the doors, retaking their posts.

The entry way resembled a fancy hotel lobby with a white couch and chairs on a plush square of red carpet around a grey stone fireplace to her right, and a bar with a grand white piano to her left the floors were black shiny marble with white walls. There was a set of red carpeted stairs that ran up the middle of the room to a landing, where they split and wound up to each floor. Anon led them to a bank of elevators behind the stairs and shuffled them all into a large grey box that had been shined to appear like you were surrounded by mirrors. He pressed the number 7, and the doors whooshed closed.

Chapter 5

The elevator doors opened to a long hallway covered with plush red carpeting and white painted walls. To the right there were several floor to ceiling windows covered by red velvet drapes tied with silver cords, allowing soft natural light to illuminate the area. Between the windows were small tables with brightly colored plants atop them. To the left, there were a few large oak doors. At the end of the hallway, there were 2 guards standing in front of 2 white doors with silver trim.

Anon led them down the hallway, stopping a couple of feet in front of the guards. "Miss Alexia Vaughn has been summoned for an audience with the High Worlock." He repeated the statement from earlier, not addressing either guard in particular. The guards didn't budge, they just stood there at attention.

Just as Lexi was about to step forward and try to address the guards, one of the doors swung open. The guard standing in front of the door moved to the side and resumed his stance, staring at the wall in front of him, basically ignoring their presence.

A harried young fire mage came rushing out. He was dressed in a dark suit with a red tie that matched his hair and eyes. "My apologies, my apologies, I was just now notified of your appointment, or I would have met you at the train. I am the High Warlocks personal assistant Stephen and will be available to you if there is anything you need during your visit. Please follow me. He is expecting you."

With that, Stephen turned on his heel and rushed back inside. Tia giggled and Max gave a snort of annoyance. "You would think someone had set fire to his ass the way he rushes about."

Max's dry statement caused laughter to erupt from Tia. Lexi just shook her head and entered the council chambers.

Anon stayed with them as they entered the large room. It had rows of seats on either side of the walkway and a raised dais where the High Worlock sat with his assistant on one side and his future successor on the other. There was a large, brightly colored tapestry hanging from the wall behind them. It showed Night City. In the center, there was a heart that had what appeared to be shops and things inside. Below that, there was a transportation hub that showed trains and boats and flying machines. On the right side, from the bottom to the top, there were 3 castles labeled Shifter's Den, Circle of Magi, and Nights Children. There was a slightly bigger castle at the top labeled Grand Council, with 2 castles going down to the left Miners Town, Fae Folk, and what appeared to be a large pond labeled The Grotto.

The High Warlock sat centered in front of the tapestry. He was a large, muscular man only a couple of years older than her father. It took all of Lexi's willpower to hold onto the formalities and not throw herself at him.

The High Warlock was one of her father's oldest friends. As a powerful healer, he had been assigned to her dad's unit during his younger years and they had been through much together. He was like an uncle to her he was always there for special occasions and holiday dinners. She absolutely adored him, and she was certain he felt the same. Lexi reigned in her need for his comfort and bowed with the others, making sure she kept her head lowered and eyes on the ground at her feet when she straightened. Lexi hated the formalness of the situation but complied, nonetheless.

"So, Lex, I am guessing your arrival caused the excitement earlier. Am I right?" The high warlock grinned down at her with a twinkle in his eye. "Enough with the formal crap," he said, rising from his chair and moving to stand in front of her.

Lexi met his eyes. "You did that on purpose, didn't you?" she accused, placing her hands on her hips and pouting a bit.

Everyone but Max and Tia took in a sharp, surprised breath. One did not accuse the High Warlock of anything, ever. He laughed, throwing his head back. "You know damn well I did. I figured it would be an excellent test to see how things were handled and I have to admit the response time was wonderful. However, the way it was handled was not to my liking." He shook his head in annoyance. "Aside from Mr. Bright," he said, nodding at Anon behind her. "The whole thing was a shit show and handled at an embracingly horrible level. That mage should have NEVER pushed that panic button. He didn't even speak to you, just took one look and bam instant party," he said throwing his hands up in exacerbation.

"Uncle, you can't exactly blame him," Lexi responded. "I mean, you know how people feel about me."

"Excuse me. Did you say uncle?" The successor stood looking between Lexi and the High Warlock.

"Yes," they said in unison.

The High Warlock turned and addressed the two other men in the room. "Alexia Vaughn is the daughter of my oldest friend, Commander Byron Vaughn. I have known her since she was born. So yes, I am in all respects her uncle." He turned away from the men dismissively and pulled her into a hard hug. "I am sorry if you were frightened, but I needed to know how things would play out if a Transcended ever came here for help."

Lexi relaxed into him, returning his hug. "I know, uncle," came her muffled reply. "It's just been a long couple of days." Lexi sighed and pulled back.

He gave her a soft pat on the cheek and turned to Max and Tia. "I should have known you two would be here, too. I am glad to see you both." He opened his arms in invention and Tia immediately bounced into them, giving him a warm hug.

Max waited until she was done and held out his hand for a more reserved greeting. Max wasn't one that liked to be touched. The only one that could really touch him without making him feel uncomfortable was Tia. The High Warlock gave his hand a firm shake and nodded his head at him in understanding.

"Mr. Bright," her uncle said, addressing Anon. "Your command of the situation was exemplary. I trust you to educate the 2 men that did not comply with your disarm order and I will deal with the issue of the mage. I am grateful to you for personally escorting Lexi and her friends, ensuring their safe arrival." He shook Anon's hand.

"Thank you, Sir," Anon said, bowing low. "I apologize for the delay and any distress my men may have caused." Anon straightened and looked at Lexi. "If you or your friends need anything, please let me know," he said. Returning his gaze to the High Warlock,

Anon continued, "With your blessing, I will return to the keep."

Lexi watched her uncle nod at Anon. Who gave her a quick glance before he turned on his heel and left the room.

"Well Lex, it appears we have much to discuss. You have gotten yourself into quite the pickle." Her uncle moved to a door to the left of the dais. "Stephen, have lunch brought to the meeting room. Anders, Max and Tia, please join us."

They all entered a smaller room with an oval oak table in the middle. It had comfortable plush chairs surrounding it and was lit by a high window. There was recessed lighting for when discussions occurred or continued throughout the night.

They all shuffled in and took seats. "Lexi, Max, Tia, please meet Jacob Anders, my successor. Jacob meet Alexia Vaughn, Maximilious Varous III, and Mylitia Abberwood." They all said their hellos.

A group of mages shuffled in, setting platters onto the table and leaving as quietly as they could with Stephen fussing over them. The table was set with shiny translucent rainbow-colored plates, bowls and chalices with polished silver utensils. The food smelled amazing, and Lexi was embarrassed when her stomach growled loudly.

"Well, on that note, dig in everyone don't be shy," the High Warlock said as he started piling food onto his own plate. They didn't need to be told twice and in no time, everyone had plates piled high and goblets filled with fizzy drinks. Even Stephen, who went almost unnoticed at one end of the table, had a plate overflowing with food.

Chapter 6

After everyone had eaten, the High Warlock asked Lexi to tell him what happened and show off her new jewelry so that everyone could see. She felt a bit like a novelty on display.

"Your father was right. It is a tracking charm and can only be removed by the person who marked you... or their master," he announced.

Lexi looked up at her uncle. "Their master? I thought non magi biters had no master."

Jacob took a sharp breath. "Do NOT, under any circumstances, use that term in Night City again. The term biter is a derogatory word used to describe the night children, and they do not approve. If you are heard using it, you might find yourself beaten or even killed," he said anger lacing his tone.

Lexi swallowed. "Sorry, I didn't mean to offend."

Jacob waved his hand in a dismissive gesture. "I take no offense. However, Stephen will provide you with a list of similar terms, so you don't repeat the mistake," he responded.

"Thank you, Jacob," the High Warlock said, raising an eyebrow at him. "All Vampyres have a master. The Royal House of the All-Seeing Eye is presided over by a king and queen of sorts. They are pure-blooded Vampyres and, in that respect, masters of everyone in their coven. There are 6 covens, each with a pure blood pair as their head. These pure bloods make up the Night Council. You will make your appeal to just one coven. Nonetheless, if necessary, I will petition the Night Council in hopes that they will overturn any negative decision."

Her uncle assured her, handing her an envelope with her name scrawled across it in a fancy script.

Lexi's hand shook slightly as she reached across the table and took it, folding open the parchment inside to reveal a handwritten summons.

Alexia Vaughn
You are hereby summoned to appear
in front of the Imperial Masters of the
House of the All-Seeing Eye.
You will arrive promptly at midnight
and remain for one hour.

In smaller print at the bottom it read, please note proper etiquette guidelines and attire have also been provided.

Lexi read the note out loud for everyone to hear.

"Attire?" Tia asked. Ever the fashionista.

"Yes, a box arrived with the summons. It has been placed in your suite," Stephen answered Tia.

She made an excited noise. "I can't wait to see," she squeed.

Stephen shook his head, handing Lexi a larger piece of parchment. "Sorry miss Abberwood, you will not be going."

Tia pouted as Lexi read aloud from the new paper.

RULES AND ETIQUETTE

You may arrive at the main gate no earlier than 11:55

You may have 1 driver drop you off at said gate and return no earlier than 12:55

You will enter the gate unaccompanied. An escort will be provided upon entry. Said escort will remain by your side for the entire hour. Once the hour has passed, you will no longer be the escort's concern unless an extension has been agreed upon.

You will wear the ensemble provided. Said ensemble will be yours to do with as you wish after you leave the Night Children's circle.

The Night Children do hereby proclaim that you will be protected from harm during the hour provided and will be returned to the main entrance of the circle in the same condition in which you arrived.

Max's expression had grown dark, almost stormy. "You mean they want her to go alone?" he growled. "She's not going." Max crossed his arms and glared at the offensive paper.

"She has no choice," The High Warlock replied softly. "This is a summons, not an invitation. That bracelet marks her as one of their Coven and if she tries to refuse, the consequences could be deadly."

Lexi took a deep breath and let it out. "I will be ok Max. They said I will be returned safely," Lexi said softly.

"She's right. The enclosed rules are, in fact, a binding contract." Jacob was looking between Max, Tia and Lexi with an odd look on his face.

Her uncle caught the look and chuckled. "These 3 have been friends since primary school. Max is very protective and tries his best to keep them from doing anything too crazy." His successor just nodded and folded his hands in his lap.

"Well, I guess it would be best if we had Stephen show you to your suite." Her uncle winked at her, and Lexi groaned.

No doubt it was lavish: he loved to spoil her when he came to visit, and she had no doubt he would do the same now. "A suite uncle?

Really? You know that simple rooms would be more than adequate." Lexi shook her head at his beaming smile.

"The suite has 4 bedrooms with a living room and kitchen so that you will be able to meet in private. I will come and see you tomorrow afternoon. Stephen, escort them, then meet me in my office, please." He stood, putting an end to any arguments.

Jacob and Stephen stood with him. Lexi and her friends did the same, making sure to collect the papers on the table. Lexi watched her uncle turn to leave. "Uncle, it is nice to see you. I have missed you and thank you for all of this. I know you are doing a lot for me, and I want you to know that I understand that." The thanks came out a bit awkward, but Lexi was sincere.

The High Warlock turned back to her. "I know, Lex, and I hope we can come to a quick resolution of your problem so that we can spend some time together. You are one of our circle and deserve no less than our best efforts to help you. The fact that you are my niece is just a bonus." He opened his arms and Lexi rushed into them for another warm hug before allowing him to leave with Jacob on his heels.

Stephen cleared his throat. "If you will please follow me," he said, rushing out of the meeting room and back into the chambers.

Tia and Max were the first to follow him and, as Lexi cleared the doorway, she heard the heavy doors to the hallway opening. Stephen was apparently in a hurry.

He had already called the elevator and was waiting impatiently for them to join him inside when they entered the hallway. "Man, he's fast," Tia mumbled.

Max just grunted. When they joined him in the elevator, Stephen gave an impatient stab to the button for the eleventh floor and bounced on his heal watching the numbers climb.

"Perhaps you could slow down just a bit. This is our first time here and we don't want to get lost," Lexi said.

Stephen gave her a sideways look. "No chance of that," he said just before the doors opened and he bounced out into a very short hallway with a door at the end.

"Here we are, your suite," he said, opening the door with a brass key and stepping inside.

The suite was massive, apparently taking up an entire floor of the castle. There was a small table by the entrance with an envelope for each of them on top. The entry opened into a huge living area that had the same black marble floors as downstairs and the same style of stone fireplace with plush chairs and couches atop purple carpeting this time. There was floor to ceiling windows making up the wall to the left covered by thick purple drapes. As they walked through the room, Lexi could see an arched hallway to the right.

"I will leave you to explore," Stephen said as he turned for the door. "Your driver will be here at 10:30 sharp. If you need anything, there is a phone in each room with a list of numbers to call mine is the first one listed." The door closed behind him with a soft snick before any of them could say bye.

They did indeed take their time exploring. The suite had a modern kitchen with any appliance they could need and was fully stocked. There were 4 large bedrooms, each with a large bathroom that held huge tubs and showers. Each room had a label on the door with a name and linens in their respective colors. The one marked Alexia was decorated with purple and silver. Lexi found a black box tied with a silk ribbon on the massive four-poster bed. She opened the box to reveal a shimmering purple dress. The fabric appeared to flow like water and caught the light, making it almost glow lightly. Lexi's cheeks burned when she picked up the flimsy black undergarments that were made from the same silky flowing fabric that had a lacey pattern to them. There was a pair of heels inside the box, too. They would add about 4 inches to her height, and she was sure her feet would be screaming in pain as soon as she put them on. Lexi hung the dress and felt the day's stress take over. She decided a long hot bath might help her relax, then maybe a nap, but first she had to call her dad and give him the rundown of her day so far.

Chapter 7

Lexi woke from her nap feeling refreshed. For once, she hadn't had the bad dream. She slid on a pair of sweatpants and oversized t-shirt and padded barefoot down the hallway to investigate the smells coming from the kitchen.

Max was an excellent cook and was standing at the stove cooking some sort of stir-fry. Tia had set the table with the same rainbow-colored cutlery and silver utensils.

"Smells great," Lexi said, joining Tia at the table.

"How was your nap?" she asked.

"It was great, no nightmare this time," Lexi replied, sipping the soda that was in her goblet.

"You have been having nightmares? About what?" The concerned look on Tia's face warmed Lexi's heart.

"It's nothing to worry about. I have been dreaming about being in a dark place with the... Vampyre...." Lexi barely caught herself before she said biter. "We are in a dark place and he's chasing me, trying to make me his pet. I always wake just as he sinks his teeth in, feeling groggy and out of it."

Max joined them, spooning stir fry and rice into their bowels. "Sounds to me like it's more of a telepathic link than a dream," he said, taking his seat. "You may want to mention it to them when you have your meeting."

Lexi nodded, taking a bite of her dinner. The flavor exploded in her mouth. It was to die for. "Amazing as always," she complimented him after she swallowed.

They all cleared their plates, Tia and Lexi insisted on doing the dishes while Max went to the living room to give them some space. He was great at knowing when they needed girl time.

"I'm surprised this place doesn't come equipped with a full staff," Lexi mused as they put the last dishes away.

"It did, but they were so jumpy Max dismissed them," Tia responded with a shrug. Not bothered in the least.

"Want some help?" Tia asked, knowing Lexi hated to dress up.

"Yes, please," Lexi said. Leading Tia to her room. There was an old-fashioned dressing screen in the corner, and Lexi took the dreaded ensemble behind it. She was tempted to wear her own undergarments but was unsure if they had some way of knowing if she didn't comply with their wishes. She just sighed and gave in, putting everything on. The fabric was soft where it kissed her skin and felt amazing to touch. The dress was short and flowed down her body, brushing the tops of her thighs.

Lexi came around the screen and did a small twirl for Tia, who whistled. "Wow! That dress is OMG! Amazing!" Tia squeed. "OK. Now for the hair," she said, snapping her fingers. Lexi's hair went up into a beautiful bun with soft curls on either side of her face.

"Nope," Lexi said. "That just says bite me."

Tia snapped her fingers again and Lexi's hair formed itself into soft, long curls. "Pretty, but not right for that dress," Tia sighed and tapped her chin. "Oooo, I know!" Snap Lexi's hair went into some sort of half up, half down configuration. It had formed into an up do with curls coming out of it and streaming down her back. Tia smiled, "That's the one," Tia beamed. Then she sat Lexi in a chair at a large makeup table. "I still prefer to do the make-up the old-fashioned way," Tia explained as she started fussing over Lexi's face. She sprayed Lexi's hair with something that glittered. "You look like a princess." Tia breathed as she examined Lexi's nails and turned them different colors, deciding on clear with purple tips, "Ok, where are the shoes?" she asked. "I want to see the total effect."

Lexi complied, slipping the shoes onto her feet and standing. To her surprise, they felt amazing. She felt like she was walking on a cloud and had absolutely no balance issues.

"Come on," Tia said, grabbing her arm and pulling her out of the room. "I want to see the look on Max's face when he sees this."

Lexi let Tia drag her to the living room where Max was reading. He looked up as they entered, and his jaw dropped.

"Lexi, is that you?" he asked, getting up from the chair he was in.

Lexi giggled and did a twirl in answer.

"Wait!" Tia exclaimed, rushing off toward the bedrooms. Returning a short time later, holding a small purse and the retractable necklace.

Max took the necklace from Tia and helped Lexi put it on. Lexi took the purse and gave Tia a confused look.

"There isn't any reason for me to carry this," she said.

"Yes, there is," Tia replied, handing her the envelope that had been on the entrance table. "We are going dancing," she said with a pointed look to Max.

Max sighed and sat back down, not saying a word. Lexi shook her head and opened the envelope to find a key for the room and a charge card with her name on it. There was a bit of cash in a smaller envelope with a note from her uncle.

Lex, I expect you to find some time to have fun while you are here and what your father doesn't know won't hurt him.

xx
Uncle Augie

She smiled softly at the note and placed the other items, her phone and the summons, into the purse.

"Where did you get this?" Lexi asked, examining the purse. It matched her dress and had a nice long strap. She placed the strap across her body, allowing the purse to rest on her hip.

Tia beamed at her. "It was in the box. It must have been under the shoes," she said nonchalantly.

Lexi frowned a bit. She didn't remember the purse being there. Tia insisted on a picture and made Lexi pose in front of the fireplace.

A soft chime sounded throughout the suite, and Max left them to answer the door. He returned a short time later with Anon.

"Your driver is here," he said, returning to his seat.

As Anon entered the room, he froze. "Holy Shit," came out of his mouth before he could stop it. He turned red but didn't take his eyes off Lexi.

"Careful there, big boy, you 're starting to drool," Max growled at him.

"S-sorry, it's just you look WOW!"

Lexi blushed and did a twirl as she had done for Max. "Thanks," she said softly. "You don't look too bad yourself."

She looked him up and down. He was wearing a silver shirt that was almost transparent and not skintight but close enough to show off his broad muscular shoulders and tapered nicely into a pair of black leather pants.

"Shall we go?" he asked. "If we don't leave soon, we might not be on time. It takes at least an hour and fifteen minutes to drive there." Lexi nodded and gave Tia a hug.

Max took Anon to the side and said something in a low tone that the girls couldn't hear. Anon nodded and seemed to agree to something. He gave Tia a smile and placed a warm hand on Lexi's back, turning her to the door. Once they were in the elevator, he pushed the button marked L for lobby and pulled out his phone, sending off a quick text.

"What was that about with Max?" Lexi asked.

Anon shrugged, "Nothing," he replied, offering his arm as the doors whooshed open. She took it, smiling up at him.

Anon led her to the right as they exited the elevator and went through a white glass-paned door that led to a small driveway with a large garage at the end. Just a few feet away was the SUV from their earlier ride. Anon led her to the passenger side door and opened it for her.

"This is yours?" Lexi asked.

"Nope, it belongs to the court, but I am allowed to use it. Especially on official business." He gave her a smile making sure she was secure, then slid behind the wheel, still smiling.

Chapter 8

The ride to the Night Children's circle took an hour and 20 mins. Lexi and Anon passed the time getting to know each other. Lexi hadn't had much experience with small talk, but she was enjoying the easy banter they had going. As he zoomed off the speedway, Lexi could see the Night Children's archway.

Anon zoomed to a stop in front of it and checked the time. "2 minutes," he said, not moving. Lexi reached for her seatbelt and Anon stopped her with a warm hand on her wrist. "2 minutes," he repeated. "If you try to leave before then, you could be attacked. The rules are clear: you can't approach the desk until 11:55."

Lexi nodded nervously.

"Hey," Anon said, caressing the back of her hand. "You will be fine." His touch and quiet tone had the desired calming effect.

Lexi looked up at him and gave a shaky smile. "I know I just haven't done something like this on my own before. I have always had Max and Tia to fall back on."

Anon chuckled. "Yeah, you used to drive your dad nuts. He would regale us with tales of your adventures during lunch hour at the academy."

Lexi looked at him with wide eyes. "You were in my dad's class? Wow, what a small world," she replied.

"Yep, he is very proud of you and did his best to use you as an example of how Transcended Mages weren't a threat." He gave her hand another squeeze. "It's time. We can talk about this later if you like. I will be right here at 12:55."

Lexi nodded and released her belt as Anon came around to help her out of the car. She could see the worry in his eyes, even though he was trying to hide it.

Lexi took a deep breath and left the safety he provided, heading for the kiosk in front of her.

There was a pale girl with faded green streaks in her white blonde hair sitting on a stool flipping through a magazine. She looked up as Lexi approached. Lexi's hand shook as she opened her purse to retrieve the summons. She handed the paper to the girl, not sure if she should speak and afraid to make any sudden movements. The girl looked over the paper, then looked Lexi up and down. "Nice dress," was all she said before she returned to her magazine.

Lexi opened her mouth and closed it, not really sure how to reply to that. There was a soft chuckle that came from the shadows to her left, causing her to jump. Lexi whirled towards the sound, watching a tall, pale man melt out of the night, looking like he had just stepped out of the pages of the girl's magazine.

Once he appeared and she could see him clearly, she reevaluated her first impression. He was, in fact, average height with jet black hair and dark eyes.

He stepped into the small glowing stream of light that came from the candles overhead. "Sorry love," he said, as he stopped a couple of feet away. "Didn't mean to scare you."

The smile on his face told her he wasn't sorry at all. "I am Damien, your escort for the evening." He gave her a slight bow.

Lexi nodded. "Alexia," she replied. For some reason, she was afraid that giving him her nickname would make him more familiar with her and she wanted to keep as much distance as possible between them. Physical and otherwise.

His smile was cold and unfeeling when he looked at her. It made goosebumps appear on her arms. He was definitely a predator, and she was prey. "Shall we?" he asked, gesturing toward the entrance of the Night Children's circle.

The first thing she noticed when she entered was the statue. It loomed high into the night from the center of the circle. The only thing you could make out were the facial features of the intertwined couple. They appeared to be smiling down on her from their towering height, their faces bathed in moonlight.

"The Eternal couple," her escort supplied. "They were the first Vampyres brought into this realm." He seemed satisfied by her surprised reaction.

"What do you mean, brought to this realm?" Lexi asked as she rushed to catch up to him.

He was heading to the castle, to the right that had tapestries and flags lit by soft lights marking it as the House of the All-Seeing Eye. The other castles all had similar tapestries, all with different symbols and colors.

"The Night Children were brought here by the Transcended over 3000 years ago," he said nonchalantly.

Lexi could feel the pleasure he got from dropping the news.

"Six couples in all, that make up the Night Council, each presiding over their own coven. The first couple are from our own house. You will be meeting them shortly." He gave a toothy grin as they reached a heavy door, and he held it open for her.

The inside of the castle was lavishly adorned with soft grey and purple furniture. The tables were topped with what appeared to be glass or crystal, giving the goblets that sat on top the appearance of floating in midair. There were dozens of Vampyres milling about, all dressed in the finest clothing she had ever seen. Several pairs of eyes turned toward her and seemed to take note of the bracelet she wore. Lexi wasn't sure if the distaste she saw was for her or the bobble, but it was clearly evident wherever she looked.

"DAMIEN!" The loud roar made everyone turn toward the stairs in the middle of the room. In a blur, the man that had been standing on the landing was in front of her.

Damien gently took her arm and moved her behind him, much like Max with Tia.

"WHAT are you doing with MY pet?" The man was shorter than Damien, with a white suit and curly blonde hair. Lexi couldn't see him well, but she knew he was definitely the one that had marked her.

"As you well know, Marcus, your pet has been summoned to appear before the Imperial Masters. I have been chosen as her escort," Damien's response was deadly quiet.

"I will escort her. You are relieved." Marcus gave him an impatient wave of his hand, trying to step around Damien.

Damien smiled a deadly, fanged smile and punched Marcus, sending him sprawling across the floor to land at the feet of a bored-looking couple. "You will not address me as if I am your lesser, cousin," he spat out. "I have been bound to this task and you will not attempt to break my oath. We will be having words about this later. I will not be responsible for keeping the Masters waiting."

With that last statement, he grabbed Lexi's arm. Only slightly loosening his grip when she cried out in pain and led her to the elevators. Once inside, he pressed the button for the 7th floor. He waited until the doors were closed before he released her.

"I apologize if I hurt you," he growled out, his mood obviously darkened by the exchange downstairs.

"It's ok," she replied, her voice barely audible. She was immensely thankful that he hadn't handed her over. She was positive if Marcus got his hands on her, she wouldn't live long. The doors whooshed open, revealing a hallway lit with candles. It resembled the same hallway that led to the council's chamber in the Circle. However, this hallway had no windows and was decorated in purple and silver.

There was no guard at the door. Damien walked up to it and knocked so lightly she couldn't hear it. A short while later, the door was opened by a tall, pale grey-haired butler.

Damien entered the room, and Lexi followed. The only visible furniture in the room were 2 large black thrones in the center on a raised dais, containing an unmoving couple who were in appearance not much older than her. They had white, almost glowing hair and matching purple robes. There were about a half-dozen people milling about the room, holding quiet conversations.

"Alexia!" came a soft excited squee from the female on the throne. She gave a bright smile and seemed to come alive in her chair.

Lexi bowed low and averted her gaze, as she had been taught to do.

"Now, now, we keep eye contact here," the girl chided.

Lexi immediately straightened, blushing a bit.

"That's better," she cooed as she got up from her throne and seemed to glide down from the dais, coming to stand in front of Lexi.

"Britt," came a deep, chiding tone from the guy sitting on the other throne. "She is here to make a petition, not audition to be your new pet." Britt returned to her throne, pouting a bit.

"She would make a lovely addition to my collection." She sighed.

The butler opened the hall door and closed it again behind an angry-looking Marcus.

"Good, now that we are all here, let us begin," the man on the throne said, giving Marcus a warning look and stopping him from getting any closer to her.

A girl a couple inches taller than herself, looking like she had just walked off of some runway, appeared in front of the dais and the rest of the room immediately grew silent.

"We have been gathered tonight to review the removal of marking petition set forth on behalf of Alexia Vaughn. Miss Vaughn will step forward and stand in the immobilization circle." She pointed to the circle and Damien gave a light push to Lexi's lower back, indicating that she wasn't moving fast enough.

Lexi hurried to comply, stepping into the circle and feeling the loss of control as soon as she was all the way inside. She took a deep breath and found that she could turn her head slightly, but that was the only movement the circle allowed.

Damien took up a post behind her, barely visible from the corner of her eye.

"The petitioner's master will stand in the opposite circle," the woman said indicated a circle a few feet away from Lexi, and looking at Marcus, who sneered.

"I will not be held immobile like a piece of cattle," he growled at the girl.

The man, who she still had no name for, shot up from his throne, his grey eyes flashing as he leapt through the air and landed in front of Marcus with a snarl. "How dare you show such disrespect!" The man grabbed him by his curls and dragged him into the circle, forcing him to kneel with his face on the floor. "At the conclusion of this hearing, you will be properly disciplined." The man growled the words as he returned to his throne.

Once he had settled himself on the seat, he nodded at the girl who hadn't moved from her place in front of them and she continued as if there had been no outburst.

"Alexia Vaughn, you have petitioned the House of the All-Seeing Eye for a removal of marking. Is this correct?"

"Yes," Lexi answered, feeling as if she had no choice. The word was forced from her lips.

If she had wanted to give any other answer, she would not have been able to.

"That feeling you just had was the compulsion circle. You will be forced to answer any question put forth to you without hesitation and in full truth," the woman said barely sparing Lexi a glance.

"I hereby bring these proceedings to order presiding over the issue at hand are the Eternal Couple Britania and Zachariah Vanderblood Masters of the House of the All-Seeing Eye," she said.

"Miss Vaughn, please explain to the court how you became marked," she said, sounding bored.

Lexi immediately heard herself recant the events that led to her marking. She would have liked to add more but couldn't. Apparently, the circle only allowed her to give relevant facts to the question asked.

"I see," she said, turning to where Marcus knelt.

"Margus Hunt, is this recounting factual?" she asked.

"Yes," came the muffled hiss.

"Did you recognize miss Vaughn before you attacked her?"

"Yes."

"If you had caught miss Vaughn, would you have bitten her?"

"Yes."

"Hmm, and were you aware that Mistress Britania had forbidden capture, turning, or any other interference in miss Vaughn's future until she deemed otherwise?"

"Yes."

"Why did you attack her, then?"

"I wanted her for my own."

"Do you recognize the Eternal Couple Britania and Zachariah Vanderblood as your masters?"

"No."

Everyone in the room inhaled a shocked breath, including Lexi. Murmuring could be heard behind her as the shock of the statement took hold.

"The court will be silent," Zacharia's powerful voice rang through the room, causing silence to once again descend.

"Thank you, master," the girl said, returning to her task.

"If you do not recognize the Eternal Couple Britania and Zachariah Vanderblood as your masters, who then do you serve?"

"No one, I am my own master."

"I have heard enough," Britt said in a cold, angry voice. "Zach?" she asked, gazing lovingly at her mate.

Zach nodded at giving her hand a soft kiss before he rose and moved in front of Marcus.

"Marcus Hunt, you are hereby stripped of any holdings you may own. You are no longer a member of the house of the All-Seeing Eye. You will be held in the dungeons pending judgement from the Night Council." Zach reached down and removed the bracelet on

Marcus's wrist. It was an exact copy of the one Lexi wore. "Remove him," he ordered to no one in particular.

At the command, 2 guards emerged and stood Marcus in the circle. They placed large manacles on his wrists, then dragged him from the room.

Zach returned to the dais and kneeled at Britt's feet, taking her hand in his and placing the bracelet on her wrist.

Lexi gulped. She now had a new master.

Britt beamed at Zach. "Thank you love," she breathed, leaving her throne to walk around Lexi inspecting her new possession.

Britt stopped in front of Lexi. "I release you from the circle," she said in her melodic voice.

Lexi felt Damien's hand on her arm as he pulled her out of it.

"The court is dismissed. This is now a matter between master and slave," Zach announced. Everyone that had been standing around immediately exited through the door held by the butler.

The only one who didn't leave the room was Damien. "Mistress," he said with a bow. "I am bound to protect miss Vaughn and cannot leave her side."

Britania waved her hand at him dismissively. "Fine, fine," she said absentmindedly.

"Alexia, you may speak freely with no fear of offence," she said, turning and bouncing back to her throne.

Lexi tilted her head in thought. "What exactly does this mean?" she asked, holding up her wrist with the bracelet.

Britt smiled at her, showing her fangs. "It means you have been marked as property and belong to the one that holds the matching bracelet. Once you are marked, you can't be bitten without your owners' permission. If a Vampyre should try, they would turn to ash. If your master were to give you a direct order, you would have to comply. For example, cluck like a chicken and flap your arms like little birdie wings," she said.

As soon as the order was given, Lexi started to cluck and flap. She wanted to stop but couldn't control her own body.

"Stop," Britt ordered, and Lexi immediately stopped returning to her previous position near Daimen.

"That sucked," she blurted without thinking, causing Britt to giggle.

"Yep, we try to avoid marking people. Marcus should have never been in the wood, let alone marked you. However, I see this as an opportunity. We need your help." Britt met her eyes, all fun gone from her expression.

"What in the world could I help you with? I mean, you guys have every kind of mage imaginable, plus your own abilities."

Britt gave a wistful smile. "I wish to have a child." The soft, longing answer knocked the air from Lexi's body.

"And, um, how do I fit into that plan?" Lexi asked, terrified of the answer.

"If I wish to conceive, I need to drink a special potion. There are 3 ingredients that you will procure," Britt replied.

Lexi took a relieved breath, glad it wasn't something else they needed from her. "What are the ingredients?" she asked curiously.

Britt clapped her hands excitedly, taking Lexi's curiosity as acquiescence. "Dragon Scales. Before you say it's impossible, there is one that lives in the caves in the middle of the Red Desert. A feather from a black Pegasus. Found in the mountains they call Rolling Hills. And lastly Night Wing fangs found in the Black Forest."

Lexi's optimism faded, taking on one of these tasks would be considered a suicide mission, let alone all 3 together. "Thats impossible," she breathed.

"We have faith that you can do it," Zach replied quietly. "We are willing to sign a contract agreeing to release you from servitude if you provide the ingredients. We will have a contract drawn up and sent to your council. If you agree, you will sign it and have it returned. If you do not, you will become the hunted and any of our children that see you will turn you. Once turned, you will have to endure 100 years of torture before a petition to become a servant of the house can be filed," he said. His voice cold and expressionless.

Lexi nodded. "And what about the nightmares?" she asked.

"Explain," came Zach's curt reply.

She did, with as much detail as she could remember. He nodded. "So long as you accept your contract, those will not be an issue."

"I still don't understand why you need me." Lexi looked from Britt to Zach.

"Well, dear, you're a living transcended and have a lot more power than you let on. All of our transcended have been bitten or are too young and don't have the power needed to complete these tasks," Britt shrugged, seeming a bit bored by the conversation.

Lexi nodded quietly.

"If you have no further questions, time is running short, and we need to deliver you back to the entrance," Zach said.

"I am done for now," Lexi said.

At a nod from Zach, Damien turned her towards the exit with a hand on the small of her back. "We must hurry," he said, rushing her out of the room and into the elevator.

Lexi gave him a puzzled look. "But I am still marked," she said, holding up her wrist.

He grunted at her lack of understanding. "The rules are clear if you are behind our walls when your time expires, you are free game. If you make it to the exit, you are then safe."

Chapter 9

Damien returned her to the entrance on time, barely, but on time, nonetheless. Anon was waiting, leaning on the SUV with his arms folded and legs crossed in front of him. The sight of his familiar face made her smile. While she didn't feel like she had been in danger per se, the safety he portrayed was like a warm blanket to her nerves, and she was very happy to see him. She had only been inside an hour, but it felt more like a day.

Lexi thanked Damien and rushed towards Anon. He stood up straight as she approached. "How did it go?" he asked, taking her hand and inspecting the bracelet.

"I am still alive." she said with a shrug. "I have to complete some tasks before they will remove the mark. A contract will be sent for me to review and sign." She gave the short explanation as he secured her into the passenger seat of the SUV.

He slid into the driver's seat and sped off towards the speedway. "You don't need to get back right away, do you? You aren't meeting with the High Warlock until 4 pm, right?" he asked, giving her a glance.

"Yep. He said he had a lot to do and would come by my suite at 4 pm to hear about my adventure. I am free until then. Why?" she asked, giving him a curious look.

"I'd like to be there, if you don't mind," he replied.

She nodded, indicating she didn't mind.

"I also wanted to make sure that you didn't need to get back right away," he said, speeding down an exit marked Heart of the city.

He took a couple of side streets, then turned into a parking garage, cutting off her view of the different businesses teaming with people. The sidewalks they had passed were packed with people going to or from different destinations. There was a feeling of excitement in the air and just a hint of danger. Lexi could feel her own excitement growing. She was in the heart of the city, a place she had been forbidden to visit.

Anon parked in a space near the elevator, Lexi reached for her door, and he growled at her, making her jump. "I was raised to be a gentleman. Please allow me to get your door."

She nodded. "Ok."

He came around and opened her door, offering his hand to help her out. She took it and stepped out expecting him to let go, instead he laced his fingers with hers and led her into the elevator, pushing the button for the 3rd floor.

"Where are we going?" she asked.

He looked down at her and grinned. The doors opened into a dimly lit room leading to a dark glass entrance guarded by several large men in black t-shirts and cargo pants. A rhythmic thumping could be heard from behind them. The one in front of the door nodded at Anon and looked her up and down appreciatively, holding open the door for them. Anon led her into her first nightclub. She could feel the music as it thumped, making the lights jump and flash. They had entered on the bottom floor. The whole thing appeared to be a dance floor; it was packed, you could hardly see anything through the sea of people. Looking up, she could see people leaning against railings or sitting at tables that comprised the 2nd and 3rd floors. Anon pulled her to the stairs on the right, taking her up to the 2nd floor, weaving between groups of people before he stopped at a table in the back that had a couch on each side. Max was sitting on one couch wearing red leather pants and a black dress shirt with Tia in his lap, laughing at something she had just said. Tia looked amazing, as always, in a black and green plaid Mini skirt with a matching halter top. Her black suede boots were snug and stopped just below her knees. She had pulled her hair into a ponytail, letting the tight curls bounce freely behind her.

"Lexi," Max said, nudging Tia.

Tia turned to her with an enormous smile. "This place is amazing!!! How did it go? Are you ok? What…"

Max sighed. "Tia," he said in his calm deep voice. "One question at a time, please."

Tia gave him a sheepish grin and Lexi sat down on the sofa across from them. Anon sat next to her. He still hadn't released her hand.

As soon as they sat, a server approached, handing a menu to them. "I'm Mandi. I will be your server. Can I get you anything to drink?" she asked.

Tia held up her glass, indicating she wanted another of whatever fruity concoction she was drinking. Max asked for another bottle of water since he didn't drink. Anon insisted on soda since he was driving, and then it was Lexi's turn. She didn't get to go out and do things like this. She really had no idea what she would prefer, so she just ordered the same thing Tia had. Anon ordered some chips and salsa with a sampler platter, and the server scurried off.

"Well, how did it go?" Tia asked impatiently.

"Not here, love," Max said, giving Lexi a warning look. She didn't need it. She knew from experience that speaking in a public place was never a good idea.

Tia pouted. "Why not?" she asked Max in a huff.

"Because this place is amazing, and I don't want to think about my problems right now," Lexi supplied, winking at them.

Max gave her a thankful smile that Tia couldn't see.

The server returned, and she sipped on the sweet fruity drink, letting the flavor explode in her mouth. It was good, a bit on the sweet side, but she could deal. She munched on the different appetizers and chatted with the others about what other wonders the heart of the city held. After her second drink, her cheeks were feeling warm, and she was a bit giddy.

Tia got up, grabbing Lexi's hand pulling Max behind her. "To the dance floor." She ordered, not allowing any complaints. Tia led them down the stairs onto the dance floor.

Lexi was having more fun than she could remember. The four of them must have spent at least an hour on the dance floor before they returned to their table for another round of drinks. The rest of the night passed in a haze of drinking, dancing, and laughter.

Anon parked the SUV in the driveway a few feet away from the door. He got out and opened the passenger door behind him while Max did the same. Max leaned in and had Tia wrap her arms around his neck so that he could gently lift her from the vehicle. Lexi was a bit more of a struggle, she insisted she could walk.

Max turned back, looking in the open door he had just lifted Tia through. "Lexi, allow

Anon to carry you or he will throw you over his shoulder and make a scene," he said.

Lexi immediately complied, sighing deeply and letting him remove her from the vehicle. She wrapped her arms around his neck and snuggled into his shoulder. The 1st floor butler appeared and opened the door for them so that they didn't have to struggle. He helped them inside and then went to call the elevator for them, pressing the button for their suite.

When the doors opened, they came face to face with a locked door. Max apparently had done this more than once and had already palmed the key to the suite, and he opened the door without too much jostling for Tia. He winked at Anon over his shoulder. "The trick is to palm the key in the hand you're going to support her knees with before you pick her up. If you know what side the lock is on, it helps," he said.

Anon raised an eyebrow. "Do this a lot?"

Max chuckled. "My mother had a condition. She got weak and had trouble walking," Max explained, stopping in front of Tia's room. "Wait here." He slipped into the room, leaving the door open and reappearing a few moments later.

Max led Anon into Lexi's room. "Can she stand on her own?" Max glanced at them. Lexi looked tiny in the man's arms.

"Yes, I think so," Anon glanced down at Lexi.

Max nodded. "Ok stand her behind the screen." Max pointed to the changing screen in the corner and Anon complied, gently standing her up and moving around the screen.

Max was holding what appeared to be sweats and a t-shirt. Anon gave him a questioning look. Max smiled and snapped his fingers. The clothes disappeared and were replaced by Lexi's purple dress. Lexi stumbled around the screen wearing the sleep clothes. Anon caught her as she stumbled, picking her back up and moving to the bed to lay her down. He heard Max's fingers snap again, and Lexi's hair rearranged itself into a braid down her back. He lay her on the bed and pulled the covers over her, watching as she snuggled into them, falling asleep immediately.

Anon and Max exited the room, quietly shutting the door behind them. "Do you need help with Tia?" Anon asked as Max turned to the other door.

"No, I already changed her and put her in bed. I am just going to make sure she is covered. I will be right back." Max slipped into the room and was back in less than a minute. "She's out," he whispered. "There's a guest room down the hall if you would like to crash here," he offered.

Anon chuckled. The man was different than he expected. The freaky eyes and hair aside Max was fun to hang with. "No, thanks.

I have a bed waiting for me downstairs. I will see you tomorrow."

Max nodded and showed him out before going to bed himself.

Lexi woke feeling like crap. Her head hurt, her body ached, and her stomach felt like it was doing somersaults. She crawled out of bed, wondering how she had gotten into her sleep clothes. She slowly made her way to the bathroom, where she carefully showered and took some herbs for her head and stomach. After she got dressed in some stretchy pants and a loose shirt, she padded out to find coffee.

As she entered the kitchen, she saw Max at the stove making eggs and sausage. The smell made her stomach twist, and she wasn't sure if she should continue or go back to bed. Max handed her a cup of coffee and pointed to the table with his spatula. Tia was sitting in a chair with her head on her arms, trying to hide from the bright light of day. Lexi slid into the seat next to her, sipping on her coffee. Max joined them at the table, placing plates of food in front of both of them.

"Eat," he said quietly at their grimacing faces. "You will feel better."

They looked at each other with miserable expressions and did as they were told, only eating as much as they had to.

Once Max was happy and the food seemed to agree to stay in her stomach, Lexi and Tia got more coffee and moved to the living room.

The soft door chime sounded throughout the suite, and Max jumped up to answer the door before either of them could move.

Max opened the door to find Anon standing before him wearing black cargo pants and a black t-shirt. "I know I am a bit early," he said. "I can come back later if it's a bad time."

Max shook his head. "Nope. Now is fine. The girls are on their 3rd cups of coffee and appear to be feeling a bit better." He opened the door all the way, allowing Anon to proceed with him into the living room.

Lexi blushed a bit when she saw him vaguely recalling being carried in his strong arms. "Hey," she said a bit shyly, getting a snort of laughter from Tia.

She sent her friend a glare, which just had the undesired effect of causing Tia to erupt into giggles.

Anon gave Tia a raised eyebrow. "What did I miss?"

Tia's giggles were getting out of control. "Nothing," she managed to breathe out.

Anon looked at Max, who just shrugged at him, taking his seat next to Tia.

Anon took a seat next to Lexi. "How ya feelin?" he asked.

"Much better," Lexi answered, "Thanks to chef Max, we had food and coffee, and I feel almost normal."

Anon nodded. "That's good. I ran into Stephen, and he said the High Warlock will be here as scheduled."

Max nudged Tia and stood. "Well, since I dismissed the staff, Tia and I will get things together for tea," he said.

Lexi sat up. "I can help," she said.

"Nope," Max said, shaking his head and holding his hand out for Tia. "You, my dear, are a disaster in the kitchen and would probably burn down the entire castle."

Lexi huffed. "I'm not that bad." Max gave her a droll stare and glanced at Anon. "You take care of our guest, we will be in the kitchen," he said dragging Tia away.

Lexi blushed again. "Sorry about that. Did you want anything? Soda, Water, a snack?" Lexi rambled nervously. "No, I am good," Anon replied in his deep, calm tone.

They chatted comfortably about nothing in particular, waiting for the others to return. Lexi was surprised at how comfortable she was with him. People tended to avoid her and when they encountered her, they were jumpy and ran off as soon as they could get away. The hour passed quickly, and the next thing Lexi knew, the sound of door chimes could be heard.

"Anon, if you don't mind, could you get the door, please?" Max asked, carrying a tray into the room.

"Sure," Anon replied, rising from the couch.

"I can get it," Lexi said, standing.

"It's safer if I go," Anon said with a gentle restraining hand on her arm. Lexi rolled her eyes and turned to help Max set plates on the coffee table.

Chapter 10

Anon returned with the High Warlock, his successor, and Stephen in tow. Lexi gave her uncle a hug while Jacob and Stephen settled themselves into plush chairs, taking the tea and sandwiches that Tia offered. Lexi took her seat next to Anon and stirred some sugar into her tea.

"Tell us what happened and spare no detail," her uncle commanded, settling into his chair and biting into one of the sandwiches Tia gave him.

Lexi told him about everything that had happened the night before, leaving out the visit to the nightclub.

"The history of the Transcended is a highly guarded secret, and what has been divulged will not leave this room," Jacob stated as soon as Lexi had finished speaking.

"Shouldn't I know my own history?" Lexi responded, a bit angry. "I am transcended and barely know what that means. At least now I have some idea as to why my kind are treated like pariahs," she huffed, sitting straight in her seat.

Jacob arched an eyebrow at her. "What do you think the community at large would do if they knew of your history? Any and all transcended would be hunted to extinction. It's bad enough that the Vampyres think Transcended are some kind of good luck charms or something since they turn any transcended they find. The lack of information on transcended history is for your protection," he insisted.

"It's history as in, the past, meaning it happened a long time ago and the transcended living today had no part in it," she argued. "How many people have been punished for the transgressions of those that came before?" Jacob countered.

Lexi sat with her arms crossed, staring at the low table in front of her. She knew he was right, but it didn't mean she had to like it.

The High Warlock cleared his throat, looking back and forth between them. "I think this conversation can be tabled for a later date. I would like to get to the issue at hand. These tasks you have been given will not be easy to accomplish and I know you want to start right away, but I need you to wait a few days. I would like you to appear before the council during tomorrow night's meeting," he said.

Lexi looked at her uncle, surprised and confused. "Why do we need to be seen by the council?" she asked.

Her uncle just smiled and shook his head at her. "Not we, dear, just you. The others are of course invited to attend, yes that includes Mr. Bright, but you will be the one the council needs to see. As for why, you will see once the meeting starts. Until then, I suggest you do some sightseeing." He stood, indicating the conversation was over. "We will have dinner at 5 tomorrow, then attend the meeting together. I hope you all understand I would like some alone time with my niece," he said to nods and oks from everyone. "Ah, one more thing, Mr. Bright, will accompany you on your trip," he said, looking at Lexi. "Do not argue," he added as she took a breath to do just that.

Max showed them out and returned to his seat next to Tia. "Well, what should we see first? I hear the herbalists have a magnificent garden and the fire wielders have fire sculptures." He was grinning above Tia's head, who was now sitting with her arms crossed, scowling at the table in front of her.

"Maximilious!" Tia said, standing and stomping her foot, pinning him with a glare. "I will not sit here and miss out on the opportunities that the city has to offer!"

His grin turned into a full smile as he leaned back into the couch, draping an arm over each side. "Mylitia my dear, I love it when you get angry you have the cutest wrinkle in your forehead," he chuckled at her, shaking his head. "I am well aware that our first stop will be to replenish your wardrobe, then dinner and perhaps a movie. To cap the night off, we may even take a drive through the city to see what else we can find. The only question I have is will this be a 2 person or 4 person adventure?" Max looked at Lexi and Anon with a raised eyebrow.

"Well 4 obviously," Tia stated, turning to look at them as well.

"You don't have to," Lexi said in a rush, looking at Anon. "I mean, if you want to that would be great, but really you don't have to." Lexi's cheeks burned as she looked at the floor.

Anon had to bite back a smile as he watched her squirm a bit. "So, would this be a date, then?" he asked, watching her cheeks turn an interesting shade of red as she gaped at him before regaining her composure.

"No!" Lexi said, shaking her head as both Tia and Max said, "Yes!" in unison.

"No, no, it's not," Lexi said, glaring at her friends.

"I don't know, Lexi. You're out voted 3 to 1. I think the majority rules here and we should consider this a date," Anon said, causing her to gape at him.

"Wait, you want to go on a date with me?"

Lexi's confusion broke his heart a bit. "Yes, Lexi I want to go on a date with you," he said in all calm seriousness.

"No," Lexi said in a small voice, shaking her head. "Dating me could end your career, not to mention it could cost you friends and could even put you in danger. I can't date you, or anyone, ever, not even one time." Lexi got up and ran to her room, not waiting for a reply.

"Well, that didn't go the way I had hoped," Anon said, staring at the hallway Lexi had disappeared through.

"I'll go talk to her," Tia said softly, patting his shoulder as she walked by.

Max leaned forward, putting his elbows on his knees. "Sorry 'bout that. I should have known better than to push the dating thing. Lexi is terrified that if she tries to date anyone, it will ruin their lives."

"It's not your fault," Anon replied. "Hell, maybe she doesn't even like me," he said with a shrug.

"Oh, she likes you," Max said with a grin. "She just doesn't know what to do about it. There was never an issue before. Any guy that may have had even the slightest interest backed off as soon as their friends started teasing them. It's extremely rare for her to find someone that sees her for who she is instead of what she is, and it scares her."

"It doesn't hurt that you're her personal guardian. I'm sure you have done some behind the scenes protecting yourself."

Max shrugged. "Those 2 are my world. I love them both. Lexi is like a sister to me, and you can see with your own eyes how I feel about Tia. I won't let anyone hurt them if I can help it."

"What makes me worthy in your eyes?" Anon held Max's gaze and waited for him to answer the question.

"You, my friend, have never treated her as anything other than a woman. You don't flinch or shy away from her. From the moment you laid eyes on her, she has been nothing but Lexi."

Tia slipped into Lexi's room. It took her a moment, but she finally found her friend sitting on the window seat, staring out at the people below. "I'm a total idiot, aren't I?" Lexi asked as Tia approached.

"Not total, just simi total," Tia replied, getting a small smile in return. "Why not give him a chance, Lexi? He's a great guy, and it's not like he's asking you to marry him. He just wants to go on a date or two." Tia's voice was soft and calm.

"Have you been taking lessons from Max?" Lexi asked, trying to distract her friend.

"Hey sometimes my man has some good advice, and it needs to be shared and the only way to properly share it is to emulate him." Tia huffed, flipping her hair over her shoulder. "Now don't think you're going to distract me with Max. He makes an excellent distraction for sure, but right now we need to talk about you. You can't live your entire life in fear, and you can't make decisions for everyone. That man out there likes you, Lexi, and he deserves the chance to show you." Tia had taken a seat next to Lexi and put an arm around her shoulders as she spoke.

"He's a good guy Tia, I don't want him hurt because of me," Lexi said in a small voice, putting her head on Tia's shoulder.

"Then don't hurt him. Besides, hurting and being hurt is a part of life. You need to live and experience everything life has to offer."

Lexi felt Tia shrug and let out a sigh. "Okay," she said in a shaky voice. "It's just a date. I can do just a date, right?"

"That's my girl!" Tia squeed in her ear while giving her a bear hug. "Now go out there and apologize and ask him if he would still like to go on that date."

Lexi walked back into the sitting room, trying to breathe through the lump of fear in her throat.

Max, of course, saw her coming and stood to meet her part way. He leaned down and gave her a soft kiss on her forehead. "You got this," he whispered so that only she could hear, then he straightened and left to go find Tia.

Lexi took another calming breath and retook her seat next to Anon. "I am sorry." She cleared her throat. The words had come out as a horse whisper. "This whole dating thing is unfamiliar territory for me, and I am a little afraid. But if you are willing to risk it, I would love to go on that date with you."

Anon smiled broadly and barely managed to refrain from grabbing her up into a hug. "I would like nothing more than to take you on that date. If it helps, you can think of it as a group of friends going on an outing together rather than a group date."

Lexi giggled, "I think it actually does help. Having Max and Tia there will take some of the pressure off."

Lexi took a cautious breath. "On another note, do you even want to go on this trip with us? My uncle didn't even bother to ask. He just gave an order."

Anon shrugged. "I go where the council orders."

Her shoulders sagged a bit and she let out a breath, looking down. "I see...." she started to say, but Anon tilted her chin, forcing her to look him in the eye.

"I go where the council orders, but yes, I do want to join you on your trip. I was going to make the request myself. However, it appears that I don't have to."

Lexi gave him a shy smile. "I'm glad" it came out as a whisper, but with him so close, he couldn't help but hear her. "I'll go change," she said, looking for an escape she needed a few moments to process.

"And I will keep our guest company," Max said, breezing back into the room he had put on his heavy silver buckled boots and had his favorite black leather biker jacket in his hands.

Chapter 11

Lexi returned to her room to find that Tia had laid an outfit out for her. It consisted of a see-through black crop top with black low-rise jeans and black heeled boots. 3 camis had been laid next to the outfit and Lexi chose the dark purple one to go under the top. The cami didn't reach all the way to her waist, leaving her stomach exposed and showing off her belly button ring. Her father would kill her if he knew she had gotten it, but as a good supportive friend, she got hers when Tia did so that they could match. The memory made her smile. After she dressed, she grabbed her purple leather biker's jacket to match Max's and went to meet the others for her first ever date.

Anon seemed at a loss for words as she re-entered the room, noting that Tia had on an outfit similar to hers, just green instead of purple.

"Shall we?" Max asked, sliding his arm around Tia's waist and urging her toward the door, not waiting for anyone to respond.

Anon gave his head a slight shake and gave her a wolfish smile as he offered her his arm, which she took, allowing him to lead the way to the elevator.

The SUV was waiting in the driveway as usual. Anon held the front passenger door open for Lexi and she blushed and whispered a small thank you, feeling awkward. Max opened the rear passenger door for Tia, making sure she was buckled and comfortable before he shut the door and joined her in the back seat on the other side.

"Ok so shopping, do you want to hit up the main plaza where it's mostly clothing stores or are we looking for something specific?" Anon asked, looking at Tia in his mirror.

"The Plaza sounds perfect!" Tia smiled, bouncing a bit in her seat in obvious excitement.

"Ok then," Anon grinned back at her, shaking his head slightly as he put the car in gear and sped off toward the heart of the city.

It only took about 30 minutes to get to the Plaza. Anon parked in the same parking structure they had used the night before but this time instead of taking the elevator to the 3rd floor Anon led them through an archway that led to a courtyard that was surrounded by various stores with colorful clothing and items on display.

Tia stopped short. Her eyes were huge, and her mouth hung open. She had been shopping before, but she had never seen these many stores in one place.

Lexi smiled at her friend. "I believe we have found Tia's happy place."

Tia gave her the well duh look. "Um Yeah! Hello, we have a coffee shop," she gestured to the coffeehouse in the middle of the courtyard. "Surrounded by shops that have anything I could want. I may never leave."

Anon looked from Tia to Lexi. "I don't want to ruin anyone's mood, but we should probably be a bit conservative with the shopping spree since you guys are going to be leaving on an epic quest soon," he said.

Lexi gave Anon a bright smile. "Nope. Any mage worth 2 bits can do a bag expansion spell and uncle said that the suite is ours so we can leave anything we like there and if we wanted to, we could ship some things back to our village. But you bring up a good point. We need to buy things for our trip. Our first location is the Red Desert, so we should get some cool clothing and camping gear. Then we go to the rolling hills where it gets cold. Then the dark forest where it's wet," she said.

Tia's eyes glowed with excitement over the task. She loved shopping, and this was the best excuse to put her experience to good use.

"Right then, we start with camping gear," Tia ordered, heading to a store with a campsite set up in the window.

Lexi was exhausted, Tia had insisted on a setup for each trip, meaning they each had 3 backpacks full of camping gear and clothes. One was set up for the desert, one for the mountains, and one for the forest. They all also had various bags full of clothing for council meetings and city outings. Lexi was currently trying on her 7th dress, complete with heels. After putting on the dress, she stumbled out of her dressing room to twirl for Tia, who had a handful of dresses she had already picked out for herself. The tailor she had requested for the guys was leaving with a handful of cloth swatches.

"Yep, definitely in the keep pile, Tia stated as soon as Lexi finished her twirl."

Lexi smiled at her friend. "Tia, love, you have said that about each dress. If I agree to get them all, can I skip the last 3? I am starving," Lexi pleaded.

Tia pouted a bit. "I suppose so, but you have to get the shoes, too."

Lexi sighed in relief. "Ok, I will go change again and meet you at the checkout," she said as she disappeared behind the curtain of the changing room and quickly changed back into her own clothes.

She took the dresses and carefully balanced her boxes of shoes on top and stepped out of the room. The attendant immediately jumped up to help, grabbing the precariously balanced boxes and led the way to the counter where her friends stood. The cashier took her items and packed them into yet more bags. Lexi wasn't sure if she could carry everything they had bought so far. Heck, she wasn't even sure it would all fit in the car. She handed her little black charge card to the cashier once she had wrung everything up and only gave a slight wince at the total. Her uncle had told her to have fun and go shopping, so here she was doing just that. She had even found a present for her father: it was a silver barbecue set that had sword hilts, as handles the knife was even a miniature sword.

Lexi signed the slip and placed the card in her pocket, then reached down to gather her bags.

"Here, let me help," Anon said, taking most of her bags.

Lexi gave him a perplexed look. "What happened to the backpacks and bags we had earlier?" she asked.

He grinned and shrugged. "Max and I had some time to kill, so we put most of it in the car earlier."

Lexi giggled, "You mean it all fits?"

His smile widened. "Barely. When I heard that shopping was on the to do list, I requested a box truck, but the request was denied something about only being able to buy out half the plaza if there was less room in the car. Next time, I will have to push harder for the bigger truck." He winked at her, his eyes sparkling with laughter, and led the way back to the car.

Max and Tia were already there, leaning against the SUV with their bags at their feet, making out. Anon hit the button to unlock the car, causing it to chirp and Max to jump, straightening and blushing slightly as Tia giggled, burying her face in his chest.

Lexi and Anon pretended not to see anything as they went straight to the back, piling the bags they carried onto the ones already there. Max joined them, still a bit red, and added his and Tia's bags to the pile, making sure nothing slipped out as Anon closed the door.

"We should have reigned Tia in," Lexi said, shaking her head at the full rear portion of the SUV.

"Are you kidding? This *was* restrained for her," Max replied, dead serious.

"There is a pasta house next to the movie theater. Any objections?" Anon asked after they all piled into the car.

"Pasta is one of our favorite foods," Max replied from the back.

Tia and Lexi both nodded and said, "Yep." in unison agreeing with Max.

The food was amazing. They stuffed themselves and relaxed together, talking about anything and everything as the time for the movie approached. Since the restaurant was next to the theater, they were able to get their movie tickets with their meals. The restaurant even did dinner deliveries to the theater so you could sit and eat while you watched the show. Something they would remember for next time. They chose an action flick since it was Lexi and Max's favorite. Lexi enjoyed being able to let go and just be herself for a bit. Cuddling with Anon in the back of the theater, she felt normal for the first time in her life, and she liked the feeling. No one had treated her badly or ran screaming from her today. There were a few mages that had given her some extra space as they passed, but it was nothing compared to some of the other responses she had received.

"You look happy," Anon remarked as they walked hand in hand towards the SUV.

"I am. Today has been amazing. I feel almost normal," she said, smiling at him.

They reached the car and instead of opening her door, he pulled her into a gentle hug, pinning her between him and the car. "I want to kiss you," he whispered, stroking a finger along her jaw.

"Then why don't you?" She whispered back, tilting her head, almost challenging him. His breath hissed through his teeth, and he lowered his head to hers, stroking his lips slow and gentle against hers. Then, deepening the kiss, taking possession of her mouth, Lexi felt like he was staking a claim and she liked it. As her body melted into his, she wound her arms around his neck and returned the kiss with a passion she had never felt before.

Anon pulled back, breaking the kiss. "Damn woman," he said hoarsely, gently stroking her cheeks as he placed his forehead to hers. "If you keep kissing me like that, we will end up putting on our own show."

Lexi gave a husky giggle and blushed.

Max had distracted Tia as much as he could with the small shop outside of the theater, allowing the other couple a bit of alone time. But there was only so much he could do. After buying Tia a small green teddy bear, he held her hand and walked as slowly as he could towards the car. His height allowed him to see them before Tia, and he wasn't going to do anything to ruin Lexi's first kiss. The stall worked, and they made it to the car as Anon shut the passenger door. He blushed a bit at the grin Max gave him but didn't say a word.

Once everyone was buckled up, Anon took them on a tour of the city, holding Lexi's hand and making it hard to concentrate on the surrounding sights. She almost missed it when he pointed out the enormous castle in front of them, explaining that it was transcended central.

"Wait," Lexi said. "You mean there is an entire castle of transcended mages, and no one bothered to tell me?" The shock and hurt could be heard loud and clear in her voice.

Tia leaned forward and squeezed her shoulder.

Anon glanced at her. "I am guessing no one told you because if you walk through those gates, you can never walk back out. Any transcended mage who enters is stuck there. The only way to leave is to die. There is a spell that prevents teleportation. A lot of the transcended Vampyres you see come from this castle. I don't know much about it, but there are some shady deals that go on in there."

Lexi felt a little better, but she was tired of people keeping things from her.

The lights were a little less shiny for Lexi as they finished their drive. She held Anon's hand and tried to join in on conversations, smiling with her friends. Max seemed to be the only one not convinced. He kept giving her concerned glances that she ignored.

Anon pulled into the driveway and helped Lexi out of the car. "Wait here," he said as he jogged off towards the garage, coming back a few minutes later with two bellman carts, like you would find in a hotel, in tow. "There are more of these if we need them, but I think we can do it with 2."

Max laughed and took one from him. "Dude, you rock," he said as he went to load one up. They piled all the stuff on the 2 luggage carts and wheeled them to the elevator.

The doors whooshed open into the hallway, showing a butler leaving their suite. "Ahh, there you are," he said in greeting. "Sargeant Bright, the 4th room has been made up for you. Would you like help with the luggage carts?" The butler was pleasant but kept glancing at Lexi, and his wince as she stepped out of the elevator was almost unnoticeable. Lexi chose to ignore his existence and brushed past him, entering the suite. The fear on his face was almost comical as she passed him. If only everyone could be like Anon or at least be better at how they reacted to her, she could have a simi normal life.

Lexi sighed softly as she heard Max gruffly telling the Buttler that his services weren't needed, and he could go.

"Wait," Anon said, stepping in front of the butler. "Who asked you to make the room up for me?" The butler blushed a bit. "Sir Stephen said the High Warlock requested it, sir." His voice almost squeaked as he finished his sentence.

Anon nodded, taking out his phone and confirming the request had come from Stephen. "He did indeed make the request. However, make sure the staff knows that unless a request has been made by someone living in this apartment, they are not to be inside without one of us being present. Is that understood?"

The butler swallowed hard and stammered out a yes sir before sliding into the elevator.

Anon and Max rolled the carts into the hallway where their rooms could be accessed. They divided their bags into 4 piles and then loaded up the 2 carts with the girls' belongings. Max wheeled Tia's belongings into her room as she followed.

Anon refused to let Lexi touch her cart and insisted on wheeling it into her room. "I am not some fragile flower, you know?" Lexi's frustrations got the better of her and she even stomped her foot as she watched him wheel the cart over to her sofa.

"I am well aware of that fact," Anon said, returning to stand in front of her. "Letting me take care of you a bit won't hurt Lexi. I know you're independent and can do everything yourself, but please let me do the things I can." He gently caressed her cheek and kissed her softly.

"Good night, Lexi I will see you in the morning." He was gone before the fog cleared enough for her to reply.

Chapter 12

Lexi woke to the smell of pancakes smiling she slid out of bed and took a quick shower, throwing on some stretchy pants and an oversized T-shirt. She snapped her fingers and her hair arranged itself into a braid down her back. She opened her door to see Anon standing there with his arm raised to knock and a cup of coffee in his hand.

He smiled at her, letting his hand fall. "Good morning," he said handing her the coffee. "Don't worry, Max made it. Apparently, the kitchen is his domain, and I am allowed to touch nothing. This includes the coffee pot."

Lexi giggled at him and took a sip of coffee. "Mmm, you get used to it." She bounced up and gave him a quick kiss, then rushed off toward the smell of food. He followed, shaking his head.

Lexi took her seat at the table, and Max slid a pile of pancakes onto her plate. He had laid out toppings in the middle of the table, and she quickly covered her pancakes with peanut butter and sprinkled some chocolate chips on top before adding maple syrup. Max

set a small plate next to her: pancakes
containing sausage.

"So," she said after washing her mouthful
of peanut buttery goodness down with the
coffee. "What did I do to deserve my favorite
breakfast?"

Max smiled at her as he placed a stack of
pancakes in front of Anon. "Tia and I wanted
you to have a good start to the day since you
have to appear in front of the council tonight."

Lexi's eyes teared up a bit. "Thanks guys, I
really appreciate it. I will be fine. This council
meeting will go smoothly, and we will be on our
way tomorrow." She squared her shoulders
and sat up a bit straighter to sell her false
confidence. "Can I have more coffee?"

Max nodded and refilled her cup, adding
just the right amount of sweetener and
cream as Lexi dug into her breakfast.

"So, what's with the separate plate for the
sausages?" Anon asked.

"I don't like the syrup and stuff to mix with
them," Lexi shrugged at him.

"I literally just saw you dip a sausage in
syrup," he said crinkling his brows at her.

Lexi paused in the middle of cutting a
pancake and gave him a well duh roll of her
eyes. "Yes, but that was my choice. It doesn't
taste right if the syrup is not added to the
sausage intentionally."

Tia giggled at the look on his face. "It's a
thing. Just roll with it," she said giving his
arm a pat.

"Max and I are planning to check out the sculptures at the fire castle and the herb gardens in the healer's castle today. Do you guys wanna go?" Tia looked from Lexi to Anon.

"Sorry I wish I could, but I have to go to the barracks. I will be busy until the meeting tonight," Anon sighed, poking at his pancakes.

"I am going to pass too. I need to call dad and pack." Lexi gave her friend an apologetic smile.

"Well, it looks like you're stuck with just me." Max looked at Tia and gave her a devilish smile.

"Great." Tia sighed. "We will most likely end up in jail before lunch," she teased back.

"Do you really think it will take that long?" He mused.

"Stop, just stop. We need to behave so that we can be there for moral support tonight," Tia chided.

"Don't worry if you get arrested. I will spring you before dinnertime." Anon winked at Max, and Tia threw up her hands.

"Lexi, a little help, please."

She grinned at her friend across the table. "Sorry, Tia, sounds like the men have this one covered."

After everyone left, Lexi called her dad and gave him a rundown of what she had been through so far. After giving him the rundown, she spent another hour talking him out of getting on the train.

Once she was satisfied her father wasn't going to get on the train, she went to pack. The bags had to be enchanted since shops were not allowed to sell pre-enchanted ones. The spell was quick and easy, and she packed each one with the designated gear and clothing. They were large to begin with. They had decided that hiking packs would make them look less suspicious. Not that their trips were a secret or anything. It was mostly to make Max and Anon feel better. A group of hikers was less likely to get attention.

Having packed her bags and set out her traveling clothes for the next day, Lexi went and took a long hot bath. After her bath, she chose a black pantsuit with a silk purple blouse to go to dinner and the council meeting. She snapped through a few hair styles before deciding to let it fall in soft waves down her back. Max and Tia came back about a half hour before she had to leave and distracted her with the descriptions of the fire art and herb gardens they had seen. Stephen arrived at promptly 4:45 to escort her upstairs. He ushered her into her uncle's parlor and left. She wasn't left alone for long. Her uncle whirled into the room shortly after the door closed behind Stephen. He was wearing his formal council robes, but it didn't stop him from engulfing her in a warm hug. Apparently, he didn't wrinkle. Lexi returned his embrace, letting the tension leave her shoulders.

"There, there, love, all is right in the world," He crooned, gently patting her back. "Would you like something to drink? Non-alcoholic, of course. No alcohol before council meetings. We learned that one the hard way." He winked at her, and she couldn't help but laugh.

"No, thank you, I am fine."

He nodded and pointed to a chair. "Sit and tell me about what's been going on with you since I have seen you last."

Lexi sat and waited for him to take the seat across from her before she told him everything, she could remember about what had gone on in her village over the last couple of years. She was finally interrupted by a servant announcing dinner.

They entered the dining room, where the table was set for two. Lexi sat in the chair her uncle pulled out, hoping dinner wasn't too fancy an affair. Luckily, the fates were on Lexi's side and dinner consisted of beef barley vegetable soup followed by chicken fried steak, mashed potatoes and corn with a brownie topped with ice-cream for dessert.

"Wow," Lexi said when the meal ended. "Please tell your chef's dinner was wonderful and thank you for having them prepare my favorites."

Her uncle waved his hand. "Nothing but the best for my favorite niece."

Lexi scoffed in mock outrage. "You mean you have more than one?"

He chuckled, "Of course not, love, you're all I can handle. Now we must go to the council meeting." He then performed a cleansing spell to make sure there were no crumbs or spots on their clothing. Once he was satisfied, he gave her a brushem (a mint that cleans your mouth) and led her to the elevator, pushing the button for 7 after she entered.

Chapter 13

Lexi was self-conscious as she sat on the dais between her uncle and Stephen, surrounded by the council in front of a small audience that seemed to be composed of the members of the councils from the other castles and her friends.

Stephen banged a gavel on the table, making her jump. "Order people order this session of the Magi Council will now begin. The first order of business is a request from The High Warlock himself regarding Miss Alexia Vaughn. Miss Vaughn, please take your place in front of the council."

Lexi stood on slightly shaky legs and stepped into the circle between the dais and the audience. She slowly turned to face the council, keeping her head high and breathing as evenly as possible. She would not let these people see her fear.

Once she was in place, her uncle stood speaking loud and clear so that no one would misinterpret his next statement. "It is my request that Miss Alexia Vaughn be offered a seat on this council." Everyone in the room inhaled a shocked breath.

Lexi barely managed to keep from reacting.

"Excuse me?" The Fire mage's representative arched his brow at her uncle. "Her kind is not welcome in our society and has no residence within the Circle."

Lexi watched her uncle smirk at him. "Not true. Alexia has a suite in this castle, thus she resides within the Circle. As for her kind not being welcome in our society, we need to change that. Transcended mages are mages and therefore should fall under our protection, thus requiring a representative on this council."

The Fire mage's eyes appeared to spark in obvious anger. "You can't expect the Magi community to accept her! Giving her a position of power just puts her in danger! This has to be some kind of joke, right?" He looked around the table as if asking the other council members for support.

"The rules are clear. Each faction of the Magi community who maintains a residence inside the Circle is to have a seat on the council, and, as such, Alexia now fits these criteria. As for her being in danger, that is nothing new. She has been in danger her entire life. Adding a title to her name will do nothing to change that." The High Warlock took his seat and waited.

Each of the other council members was having frenzied discussions with their neighbors.

Once the whispers died down, Jacob stood. "I move we put the motion to a vote," his words rang through the room, effectively killing the murmurs floating in the air.

"Seconded," the fire mage stated.

Stephen stood so that he could see the entire council clearly. "A vote has been called all those in favor?" To Lexi's surprise, a loud chorus of AYES followed. "All those opposed?" Only two council members voted no, the Fire and Earth representatives. "The AYEs have it, council member Vaughn. Please take your seat." Lexi sat heavily in the chair next to Stephen.

"Any other new business?" Stephen asked, giving a few moments for anyone to respond. "Moving on then. There are no decisions that have been held from the last meeting. If there is nothing else for the council, I will adjourn." Stephen looked around the table, but everyone remained silent.

"I declare this council meeting officially adjourned. The next meeting will commence one month from today. Please be careful returning to your castles and contact me if you would like anything added to the agenda." Stephen smacked the gavel again, causing the room to come to life. Everyone seemed to stand at once. Lexi just sat in stunned silence, watching the sea of people move in front of her.

"Lexi?" Anon was kneeling next to her where Stephen's chair had been. "You, ok?"

She gave a nod, not really sure if she was ok or dreaming or something else.

Max appeared in front of the table, his head even with hers. "Is she ok?" He looked concerned, and it took her a moment to realize he was talking about her.

"I think she's in shock." Anon's voice was low and soothing. Tia appeared at her other side and placed her hand on Lexi's where it rested on the table. A small charge went through her, making it easier to breathe and increasing her awareness of her surroundings.

"Thanks Tia." She smiled at her friend. "Guys, can you get me out of here, please?" Lexi let Anon pull her to her feet and wrap his arm around her waist. He led her to the side stairs, intending to avoid the crowd milling about the seating area.

Before they could reach the door, a Fire mage appeared in front of them. "Maximilious!! You are not leaving without at least acknowledging my existence. It was rude enough for you to come here and not say hello. I will not continue to be embarrassed by your actions!"

Max stiffened. "My name is Max, and I have no reason to endure your company, father."

Max's words were quiet but deadly as he narrowed his gaze at the man before him. "Now if you don't mind Council Member, Vaughn would like to leave so that she can research how best to serve this community. I understand your need to prioritize yourself over anyone else, so we will assume the congratulations are implied and overlook your blatant disregard for council etiquette.”

The man’s nostrils flared, and Lexi could swear she saw smoke before he swung his arm, trying to backhand Max’s face. Max caught the blow before it hit. Anon grabbed Tia with his free hand and shoved both of them into the side chamber they had occupied a few days before.

“Stay here,” he growled before he shut the door and went to help Max.

Max glanced at Anon when he returned to his periphery. “Tia?” he asked.

“Safe,” Anon replied.

Max returned his full attention to the man in front of him, releasing his arm and taking a step back. There was a small crowd around them, and more guards were entering the room.

“How DARE you manhandle me!” his father growled, heading for what Max called beast mode.

“I did no such thing. I simply protected myself from harm. You are, however, making a scene and if you continue, the guards may end up doing just that,” Max replied in a calm, clear voice, attempting to keep the outside appearance rational and calm. He was seething on the inside and wanted nothing more than to throw this man off the nearest spire.

Apparently, the comment got his father’s attention. He straightened and a mask of calm appeared on his face. He even managed to smile as he addressed the crowd.

"Apologies, my friends, just a bit of family drama, nothing to worry about. Maximilious, we must do lunch before you depart. It would be good to catch up." With that, he spun on his heel and left the room, making a beeline for the elevators.

Max and Anon exchanged confused looks and shrugs. Anon turned back to the room where he'd left Lexi and Tia, not really surprised to find them standing in the doorway watching the exchange. He was going to have to go over safety rules with them.

"You can come out now," he said.

Tia was at Max's side so fast he could almost swear she teleported. Max visibly relaxed as soon as she wrapped her arms around him. He returned her hug and nudged her toward the elevator with the other two close behind. They rode the elevator in silence, letting out a collective breath when the doors whooshed open to an empty hallway. Lexi was sure they were all expecting to see Max's father waiting for them.

Anon led the way into the living room, pulling Lexi down onto the couch next to him and wrapping her in his arms. "Hell of a night, huh?" he asked, laying his cheek on the top of her head.

"Hell of a week," she replied, relaxing into him and sighing.

"I'll go make some tea," Max said, heading for the kitchen.

"I'll help," Tia said, bouncing after Max, leaving Lexi and Anon alone.

Lexi's mind was swirling. She had been through so much and she had so much left to do. She just felt overwhelmed. A seat on the council came with responsibilities. She did not know what they were yet, but she knew they were there.

"Why would he do this to me?" she asked, her voice shaky. "My entire life, all I have wanted, was to be normal and invisible. Now I feel like a freak on display."

Anon rubbed her back. "You are not a freak. You are a beautiful person, and everyone should get to see you shine."

Max and Tia returned with tea and a tray of desserts. "Comfort food is definitely required," Tia stated as she set the tray on the coffee table.

Max passed out warm tea to everyone. "I figured we could all use some chamomile." His voice was soft, but he still had an angry air about him.

Tia gently pushed Max to sit on the couch opposite them, settling on his lap with her head on his shoulder as soon as he complied. "Now, love, how am I supposed to reach my tea?" he teased her, sliding an arm around her to keep her in place.

Tia dutifully picked up his cup and saucer, balancing it on her lap. "There you go," she said sweetly as he took a sip.

The door chime sounded, and everyone tensed. "I'll get it," Anon said, standing and heading towards the door before anyone could argue.

He returned with Stephen and the butler from the night before in tow. Stephen beamed at Lexi. "Congratulations to our newest council member. I have your latest round of books. They contain all you need to know about council etiquette and what is required of you as a member. You will need to appoint an assistant. I can set up interviews if you like. I am sure the appointment requests will start piling up come morning." Stephen kept going like a ball of energy, completely ignoring the somber mood of the room.

"I don't want an assistant. Hell, I don't even want to be on the council. What was my uncle thinking?" Lexi glared at Stephen, causing a small crack in his chipper mood.

"I thought you might need council resources and the easiest way for you to access them without all the red tape would be to make you a member of the council." The High Warlock breezed into the room, settling himself in a chair. "Sorry for not knocking. Stephen, take a seat."

Lexi sighed, setting her empty teacup on the table as Stephen perched on the edge of the nearest chair.

She looked at the butler, who was still standing just inside the room holding the heavy stack of books. "Set the books anywhere and you may go," she said softly.

He took a few steps into the room and set the books on a small table. "Pardon me, miss, but I would like to request the position of house butter." His eyes were downcast, and he appeared to be shaking slightly.

"House butter? You mean for us? You are terrified of me! You won't even look at me and you're shaking like a leaf in a hurricane," Lexi said in exasperation.

The butler lifted his gaze so that he was looking in her general direction. "Yes, miss your house, butler. A person of your stature must have staff to attend you. It would not do to have other members of the council present with no one to attend them," he countered.

Lexi scoffed, "I don't need a staff. We are capable of handling things just fine. I don't enjoy being around people that are afraid of me. It makes me uncomfortable, and my home is the last place I should feel that way."

The butler nodded. "It is understandable that you should feel this way. But your status has changed, and you will need to make some changes to accommodate this. As for our fear, we cannot overcome it if we aren't given the chance. I and the rest of the staff that I would require will do our best not to make you uncomfortable. Every change starts with a small step forward. I would humbly request this to be your first step."

Lexi blinked, a bit shocked the man was right, but she still didn't want a staff.

"You're hired!" Everyone turned to stare at Tia. "What? He's right and Lexi is too stubborn to say yes, so I did it for her. Just to be clear, the kitchen is off limits during mealtimes unless it's a hosted event."

The butler nodded, giving a small bow, the hint of a smile playing at his lips. He straightened, turned, and left the room before Lexi had recovered enough to argue.

"Tia!" Lexi shouted.

Tia held her hands up in mock surrender. "Don't 'Tia' me!" she said. "Look, Lexi, that was bigger than you think, and you will thank me for it later. Now Max and I are going to go pack unless you need us for something else?" She looked around the room, but no one said anything, so she hopped to her feet and pulled Max along behind her.

"Your friend is much smarter than she is given credit for," her uncle mused. "Now I know you're leaving in the morning, so I brought your council insignia pin."

He handed her a small jewelry box with a coat of arms pin inside. It looked like a miniature map of the Circle. "You must wear this whenever you are conducting official council business. Anyone not on the council that tries to wear it will break out into hives. Once they remove the pin, it will return to you on its own. If they try to continue wearing it, they could end up seriously injured. So, if one of your friends wants to try it on, I suggest you tell them no. Members of the council are afforded certain perks when they travel. If you need a place to stay or transportation, you can request it as a council member and cannot be denied. I would use it as a last resort. Outing yourself as a council member could put a target on your back, so be careful. Last, as a council member, you are afforded protection during travel. This means that Sargent Bright can officially accompany you," he finished.

Lexi squirmed a bit. "Thank you, uncle. I'm sorry for reacting badly. It would have been nice to have a heads up as to what you were planning, though. It did come as a bit of a shock."

He chuckled, beaming at her. "They needed you to be shocked. That helped sell it. Now they can't say you manipulated me into giving you a spot on the council. The shock on your face was obviously genuine." He sat back and nibbled on a cookie, giving Stephen a nod.

Stephen immediately took out his notebook and started making a list. "Ok, you aren't giving us much time, but I will set up interviews for assistants tomorrow morning between 8 and 10 am. I know you have a train at 11."

Lexi held up a hand and Stephen stopped mid breath. "One more day. I will give you one more day, but we will be on the train day after tomorrow."

Stephen seemed to relax a bit, if it was even possible for him to do so. "Wonderful, you have helped me immensely. I may even get some sleep tonight. Ok new plan, I will make phone calls in the morning and send you a list with an interview schedule for the afternoon."

Lexi sighed. "I still don't get why I need an assistant. I am not going to be here much and what makes you think anyone would want the job in the first place?"

Stephen gave a dismissive wave of his hand. "You're a council member now. There will be tons of people wanting a chance to influence change. I will do my best to weed out the undesirables." he said, writing something on his sheet of paper. "Thats all I have. Please read the books. Do you have any questions?" he asked, looking at her expectantly.

She shook her head no.

"Well then, we will be leaving," her uncle stated, rising to his feet. "No need to show us out. We know the way." He leaned down and kissed her on the forehead. "I know it's a lot to process, but you will be just fine, I promise." With that, he left, with Stephen trailing behind him, muttering to himself.

Lexi leaned back against Anon. "I am emotionally drained." She sighed.

"I bet. It's been a bit of a rollercoaster." Anon gave her a squeeze before helping her to her feet. They cleaned the table and let the others know about the delay before they said goodnight.

Chapter 14

Lexi woke a bit later than she meant to. She'd had intense dreams and was a bit groggy. Her morning shower made her feel a bit better. She tossed on some comfy clothes and put her hair in a ponytail, since the interviews weren't til later.

She met the others at the table. Max had gone simple with a ham and egg scramble with toast and coffee as the morning meal.

"So last night you said we've been delayed again. What for this time?" Max gave her a quizzical look over his coffee cup.

Lexi rolled her eyes. "Apparently, I have to interview an assistant. According to Stephen, it's important that I appoint one before I leave, and since it appears important, I didn't want to rush through it."

Max nodded. "I agree, and it will give me a chance to go over the staff list with our new butler."

Lexi paused mid bite. "Shouldn't I do that?" she asked.

Max shook his head. "You know me. I am particular about safety."

Tia snorted. "That's one word for it."

Lexi giggled.

"Mind if I join you?" Anon asked as Max stuck his tongue out at Tia.

"Oh geez, not another one. Lexi, we definitely have a type, don't we?" Tia groaned.

Lexi grinned and blushed a bit. "You know, I kinda like it. Not the full-bore lock you away for safety part, but I enjoy having someone who cares." Anon perked up a bit.

"You are welcome to join me, sir," Max said, starting to clear the table. Anon nodded his thanks.

"While we are on the subject of safety, you two," Anon said, waving at Tia and Lexi. "Need to listen better. If you 're told to stay put, it means stay where you're told. Not open the door or peek out of the window. When you're put somewhere, it's not just for your safety, it's to keep us from losing focus."

Lexi glared at him. "Do you really think we aren't able to care for ourselves? I may not be the battle master you two are, but I do know how to fight. I learned to use a sword when I was a kid, and Tia isn't a slouch either. She may be sweet, but she's got a mean right hook. Just ask Max. Yes, Max is our protector, but only because that's who he is. If he or you, for that matter, were in trouble, we wouldn't just sit on the sidelines and fret about it. We have a long hard road ahead of us and I am sure there will be danger and fighting. Don't think for one minute that I am not going to be in the thick of it. If you can't handle us." Lexi indicated herself and Tia. "In danger, then you should stay home."

Lexi was ramrod straight in her chair. Her eyes were sparkling, and she was breathing a bit harder than normal. In other words, Anon had hit a nerve and he could see it.

"Lexi," he said gently, taking her hand in his. "I'm sorry. I didn't mean to upset you and I am sure you're capable of taking care of yourself, but I don't want to see you hurt. Just like Max would lose it if Tia was hurt. Having you in harm's way is a distraction. I know I have to deal with the fact that you may end up in a fight but please have mercy on me and do your best to stay out of harm's way when you can."

He moved to caress her cheek and was surprised when she leaned over and gave him a gentle kiss.

"I will try, but you need to not treat me like a fragile doll. I'm tougher than I look."

Anon smiled at her. "I will try, but you have to realize I do the things I do because you're important to me, not because I think you're fragile or incapable." Lexi gave him a wabbly smile with tears in her eyes.

"Really?" she asked.

"Really," he said, kissing her again.

When she sat back, she noticed Tia and Max had left the room at some point. It still made her blush a bit.

"So, are you all packed?" she asked, searching for a change of subject. Anon laughed.

"Nope, still trying to figure out how everything we bought fits in those bags."

Lexi was confused for a fraction of a second before she realized the problem. "I could do an expansion charm for you if you like. Thats how we made everything fit."

He nodded, grinning at her. "I would very much appreciate it."

Max knocked on Anon's door so that they could go to the meeting with the butler as he and Lexi were finishing the last bag.

"Time to go," he said, poking his head in the room.

"Alright, just finishing the last bag. It's going to be a pain carrying 3 packs, isn't it?" Anon asked, buckling the bag and setting it next to the others.

"Oh, no," Lexi replied. "We will be doing the desert, then coming back to refresh and handle business before we go to the mountains. Then after the mountains, we will be back here before we hit the forest," she explained.

Anon nodded. "Well, that just makes too much sense." He gave her a quick kiss and grinned as they followed Max to the living room, where Tia was reading a book.

"Since our guys are busy, do you think you might wanna do interviews with me?" Lexi bit her lip as she waited for Tia to reply.

She was tapping her chin in that teasing I'm thinking way she does. "I suppose so... but what's in it for me?" she finally replied, with a twinkle in her eye.

"Barely a politician for a day and it's already changed, my best friend," Lexi mused jokingly. "What could you possibly want, my dear?"

Tia grinned. "Plants! We have no plants. I need plants or I might wither away." She replied, putting the back of her hand on her forehead in a dramatic gesture, sending them both into a fit of giggles.

"We can have plants," Lexi agreed. "Just keep them in moderation. I don't want to live in the jungle."

Tia squeed. "I can do moderation! Yay! Ok, let's change into something business casual and set up in the office."

A short time later, they were both settled behind the massive desk in the office with a stack of files in front of them. Stephen was sitting in the chair opposite them. He had managed to narrow down his list to 20 applicants. He claimed there were over a hundred applicants, but Lexi was sure he had exaggerated the number.

"Um, Stephen. Aren't these files a little detailed? Why in the world would I need to know their favorite foods or favorite color?" Lexi asked.

Stephen blinked at Lexi. "If you have to work during mealtimes, it's good to have someone that enjoys the same foods as you.

It makes it much simpler for the kitchen staff. You will be spending a lot of time with this person, so you don't want to pick someone who will wear colors that irritate you. Having a since of a person's hobbies and recreational activities gives you something to chat about."

Lexi nodded, a bit impressed. "Wow, you put sone serious thought into this."

Stephen gave her a genuine smile. "Thank you. It's nice to see my efforts appreciated. The High Warlock picked me because I am the best, but it's still nice to be appreciated. Now you have about 20 mins to go through those folders before your first appointment." Lexi nodded and opened the first file.

She and Tia went through each one, keeping them in order, making notes with questions to ask. They tried to be as serious as possible, but every once in a while, a giggle would escape. Some of the questions and answers were just too funny. There was one person she was interested in meeting. They were the 4th or 5th file in and most of the answers given were either 'none of your business' or 'you're kidding me, right?' Lexi wasn't sure how this person passed Stephen's screening, but she would have probably given the same answers.

The interview process was not as fun as she hoped it dragged on and her back was sore before she was even halfway through, but she managed to make it to the end. The 'none of your business' guy was at the top of her list. He had been professional and seemed like the best fit so far.

Both of the girls stood and stretched as soon as the last applicant cleared the door. "I don't know about you, but I am starving," Lexi said, looking at Tia.

"Yeah, skipping lunch was not the best idea. It is teatime, so maybe Max has a yummy snack waiting?" Without any further discussion, they gathered their notes and made a beeline for the living room where Max did indeed have tea waiting, along with mounds of sandwiches and fruits and cheeses. He was definitely the best.

"How'd it go?" he asked as he poured them their tea.

"Good, I guess," Lexi replied, piling a small plate full of sandwiches and fruit. She took the food and tea to the sidebar so that she could stand and eat. "Sorry guys, I need to stand for a bit. I have been sitting for way too long."

Tia tried and failed to agree through a mouth full of food. "We have some suitable candidates." Tia said, after finally managing to swallow the sandwich, she had been chewing. "I like Miss Nillavine the Healer. She seemed fun."

Lexi shook her head. "Fun is not the goal here. I need someone who can stand up to pressure, deal with big egos, and handle things on their own since we will be away a lot. I like Mr. Aquadox. He was the only one I saw that fit what I am looking for."

Tia wrinkled her nose. "You mean the stuffy guy that told me my asking what his favorite plant was had no relevance to how he did his job?"

Lexi nodded. "Yep, that's the guy," she replied with a grin.

"Ok." Tia shrugged. "You're the one that has to work with him."

Lexi texted Stephen, letting him know her choice. His response was almost immediate, saying she had made an excellent choice and they would arrive in 10 minutes. She groaned a bit but used the time to finish her tea. Suppressing her giggle when exactly 10 minutes later, the Buttler announced Stephen and her new assistant's arrival. She would bet good money that being even a minute late would cause him physical pain. Her new assistant was wearing a grey suit with a light blue shirt that made his tan skin stand out. His hair was streaked with every color of blue imaginable and his eyes were a dark, almost navy with aqua irises. The color seemed to flow like water.

"Shall we convene in your office?" Stephen asked, almost hopefully.

"Nope," Lexi replied, taking her normal spot on the couch. "Have a seat," she said, indicating the chairs.

Anon entered the room as the 2 men sat walking straight to Lexi and giving her a soft kiss on the cheek before sitting next to her. "Sorry if I am late. Did I miss anything?"

Lexi shook her head.

"No, just tea," Max said, having already cleared the table. "You want us to go or stay?" Max asked.

"Stay please," she replied.

He nodded, playing with a strand of Tia's hair.

"I assume we are all ready, so I will just get things going. Mathias Aquadox has agreed to take the post of assistant to Alexia Vaughn. I have taken the liberty of providing him with contact information for everyone present and given him a brief rundown of who you all are. But to put a face to the name the fire mage is Maximilious Varous III. He prefers to be addressed as Max. The healer is Mylitia Abberwood or Tia. Sergent Anon Bright, you should have at least heard mentioned around court, and of course, council member Alexia Vaughn or Lexi. Usually, it takes a few weeks to get things smoothed out between assistant and council member, but as you're scheduled to leave in the morning, we will have to do as much as we can now."

Mathias cleared his throat. "Leave? What kind of trip is this and how long will you be gone?" He posed the question directly to Lexi, looking her in the eye. His lack of outward fear for her is one of the reasons she chose him.

Lexi took a deep breath. "It's a long story, but the four of us are leaving for the Red

Desert in the morning. We don't know exactly how long we will be gone."

Mathias nodded and wrote some notes. "Unorthodox, but acceptable. With your permission, I will keep a list of those requesting your time and you can tell me with whom you would like to meet upon your return."

Lexi nodded. "Sounds good to me."

Stephen's phone rang, and he excused himself to take the call in private, returning a short time later. "I apologize, but I am needed elsewhere. If you need anything, please don't hesitate to ask."

Lexi smiled at him. "I am sure we will be fine and thank you for all of your help."

He waved his hand over his shoulder in a dismissive gesture. "Just doing my job," he replied, rushing out of the suite.

Lexi turned her attention to Mathias. "Just to make things clear, my friends never need an appointment to see me and always have priority above everyone except my uncle."

Mathias nodded. "Of course. And who is your uncle?"

Lexi smiled. "Agustus Wood."

Mathias blinked. "The High Warlock is your uncle?"

Lexi grinned. "Yep...." Before she could continue, the butler appeared.

"Mr. Maximilious Varous II." The announcement seemed to suck all the air out of the room. Max was up and in front of the group so fast Lexi could have sworn he had vamp speed. Lexi hadn't felt Anon move, but he was also in front of them, standing next to Max.

"Ahh my son, there you are!" his father crooned in fake sweetness sweeping into the room. "Rumor has it you're leaving in the morning. I thought we were going to have a luncheon before your departure. The only excuse I can come up with is you 're so busy you didn't have time to eat, so I decided I would make myself available for dinner. I do hope your staff is capable. I simply abhor meals that are unpalatable."

"Get out," Max growled, "I will not be sharing a meal with you now or at any point in the forceable future."

Maximilious sucked his breath in through his teeth. "That is no way to address your father! I knew I shouldn't have allowed you to attend that school after your mother passed. They definitely need to update their curriculum to include manners training."

Max gave an unamused chuckle. "The High Warlock didn't agree. He understood and took into account what I wanted. You had no choice, and my manners are impeccable. I will not, however, bother to use them with you. Now leave, you are not welcome here."

Maximilious's anger was starting to show. The fake smile he'd plastered on his face was fading, and his breaths were coming hard and fast. "I have tolerated your inappropriate behavior long enough! Your dalliance with the harlot is ov...."

Before anyone could blink, Maximilious Varous II hit the floor, hard. Max was standing over him, but to everyone's surprise, Mathias was between them with a hand on Max's chest.

"Mr. Varous," he said, addressing the man on the floor. "I am Mathias Aquadox. I have been newly appointed to handle miss Vaughn's schedule and any meetings taking place in this residence, personal or otherwise, must be scheduled through me." He dropped a card onto the man's chest. "This is my contact information. Please use it in the future. Now then, would you like me to call for a healer to meet you in the main hall after the guards remove you?" Mathias was busy tapping on his phone, barely giving the man on the ground any notice.

Maximilious slowly rose to his feet. Blood was pouring down his face and 2 purple circles were forming under his eyes. His nose was definitely broken. A minor commotion was heard at the door, then a group of 5 guards entered the room.

"Wonderful response time," Anon said, stepping forward. "Please remove the trash from the living room." He indicated Max's father, noting only a slight hesitation from the lead guard before he nodded to 2 of his guards. A muscular female and a shorter, husky male stepped forward, each grabbing one of Maximilious's arms, turning him towards the doorway.

"I will not be dragged anywhere!! Unhand me!!" he shouted. The guards just ignored him and drug him all the way to the elevator.

The lead guard looked around the room and gave a small bow. "Please call if you need any more assistance," he said, then turned on his heel and left.

There was a charged energy in the room after the door closed. It was like they were all afraid to breathe. Then Max laughed loud and deep, causing everyone else to join, re-leaving the tension in the room.

"Mathias, you are going to be a good fit here," Max said, clapping the man on the shoulder before returning to the couch to cuddle with Tia.

"That is, if he still wants the job." Lexi pointed out.

"Why wouldn't I want the job?" Mathias asked, confused, which made everyone erupt in more laughter.

"Would you care to join us for dinner?" Tia asked him with a gentle smile on her face.

"On any other night, I would say yes. However, tonight is an anniversary and if I cancel, Stephen would be quite put out." The matter-of-fact statement sent them all into a bit of shock. Mathias and Stephen, who would have thought?

Lexi recovered first. "Okay then, let's get this over with so that you can be on your way."

"Tell you what, I will take Max to the gym while you finish. Then, we can go out for dinner. One last trip into the city. Sound good?" Anon asked, standing and stretching.

Lexi nodded her approval.

"Would you like me to make reservations?" Mathias asked, phone at the ready.

"No need but thank you," Anon replied.

"How is it we have been here a week, and I didn't know we had a gym?" Max asked, joining Anon as they went to change.

"It's in the guard's wing and takes a special key card. I will have one made for you."

The men set off for their work out as Lexi and Tia filled Mathias in on why they had to leave in the morning and the other trips they had to take. A little over an hour later, the men returned as Mathias was leaving.

They agreed on a quiet dinner with a stroll through the enchanted park and then coffee and dessert.

Chapter 15

Lexi woke the next morning with excitement coursing through her veins. She went through her morning routine, taking a shower and braiding her hair. Her choice of travel wear was. black cargo pants and a matching tank top that left about an inch of her stomach exposed, then she made sure her dagger was firmly fastened to her calf and didn't show under her pants. She put the matching necklace on, feeling the comfortable weight of the cross on her chest. After getting dressed, she went to join the others. Max made ham and cheese omelets. Lexi was so excited she could hardly eat, but she managed to get down enough to make the others happy.

Mathias arrived as they were finishing, only agreeing to a coffee and pastry to keep Max happy. Max introduced him to the butler and other staff while Lexi and the others went through their packs one last time in the living room.

"We should probably get going," Max said as he entered the room, taking his pack from Tia and effortlessly slipping it on.

"Mathias, I am not sure if you have a place to work or not, but you're welcome to use the office here. Just let the staff know when you're here and when you leave, please," Lexi said.

He just nodded and said, "Thank you."

Lexi was glad the elevator was spacious. Five people and the large packs took up a lot of space. She was expecting to stop on the main floor and take the SUV to the train station, but Mathias held a card to the reader and pushed a button after they entered. When the doors finally whooshed open, they went to a small platform with a trolley car waiting in front.

"As a council member, you are entitled to certain perks. The trolley will take you directly to the train station where you will enter the VIP lounge to await your train's departure," Mathias said, getting them, all settled aboard and taking a seat himself. Once he was seated, the trolley sped off.

"Um Mathias? Are you going to be joining us for the entire journey?" Tia asked, a bit confused.

He smiled at her. "No, just to the train station. I have a special pickup to make."

The rest of the trip was made in silence. The trolley finally rolled to a stop in front of another platform. Lexi could have sworn it was the same one except the sign over the entrance said 'Train Station.' They all clambered off and entered another elevator, taking a brief ride up. As soon as they exited, a shrill shriek assaulted Lexi's ears.

"DADDDYYYY!!!" A small girl, not more than 6, came rocketing towards them, launching herself into Mathias's arms. "Daddy! Daddy! Did you miss me?? I missed you sooooo much." The girl rambled off at top speed, locking her arms around Mathias's neck in more of a strangle hold than a hug.

Mathias returned the hug. "Of course, my little love!"

She gave him a beaming smile. "Where's daddy S?" she asked, looking around.

"He is home making sure your gifts are wrapped properly. Now I would like you to meet my new boss and her friends. This is miss Alexia Vaughn. You may call her miss Lexi." Mathias continued down the line when he finished, he turned to them. "I would like to introduce my daughter, Amitha," he said with a blush.

"Hi," she said with a small wave in the safety of her father's arms.

"Well, Miss Amitha, it's a pleasure to meet you," Max said, giving her a full regal bow and getting a giggle in response.

Mathias seemed relieved when the chime sounded for the boarding announcement. "Have a safe trip. I will see you when you return," he said, taking a step back towards the trolley.

Tia gave a wave and a smile. "It was nice to meet you, Amitha." She bounced off towards the train with Max in tow.

He gave Amitha another small bow before entering the train behind Tia.

Anon gave the girl a wink, then went to go stand by the train's doorway to wait for Lexi.

"Well, then, Amitha, I will leave you in charge. Make sure your dad takes good care of things while I am gone." She gave the girl a wink and smile. "Mathias, thank you for everything. I am sorry I have to run so soon and just for the record. We won't pry. We all have our own stories and understand, not wanting to share them." She turned and walked to Anon, who wrapped her in his arms and kissed her before helping her up.

Lexi opened the door and whistled in admiration. They had a whole car to themselves. It had a seating area with a tv and a full bathroom with a shower and two bedrooms. There was a snack tray set out with a card from her uncle that simply read 'Safe Travels Luv Auggie. Lexi smiled at the note. She had been a bit sad he hadn't been there to see her off. This helped a little, at least.

Max and Tia had claimed one of the rooms, tossing their packs in the corner. Anon and Lexi did the same with the other than went and joined their friends on the couch of the sitting room.

"We finally made it." Tia mused. "Yeah, it's hard to believe that it's only been a week since everything went topsy-turvy. It feels like it's been months and we still have so far to go," Lexi responded as the train started its gentle rock, gaining speed and leading them to their next adventure.

About the Author

Eileen Roof was born and raised in California. She is currently living on Catalina Island off the coast. She enjoys collecting weapons and likes skulls, she loves to read and play video games in her spare time. She loves fantasy, sci fi and exploring new worlds without leaving her favorite chair at home.

9 798988 027904